D11133509

DAY OF
THE DEAD

My wife, Robina, and I have spent many years travelling in Mexico, which is a deeply magical country whose people are intensely spiritual but are often poor. Many illegal immigrants try to cross the border into the United States and are either caught or live in fear of being so. I wrote Day of the Dead *because I know that although life in Mexico can be hard, America is not necessarily the land of golden opportunity that so many Mexicans suppose.*

A.M.

Award-winning author Anthony Masters knows how 'to hook his reader from the first page' *Books for Keeps*. He is a best-selling children's author renowned for tackling serious issues through gripping stories, but he has also written extensively for adults both fiction and non-fiction. For Orchard Black Apples list he has written six *Ghosthunters* stories and two novels, *Spinner* and *Wicked*. He lives in Sussex with his wife and has three children.

ANTHONY MASTERS

DAY OF THE DEAD

ORCHARD BOOKS

ORCHARD BOOKS
96 Leonard Street, London EC2A 4XD
Orchard Books Australia
14 Mars Road, Lane Cove, NSW 2066
First published in Great Britain in 1998
© Anthony Masters 1998
The right of Anthony Masters to be identified as author of this work has been
asserted by him in accordance with the Copyright, Designs and Patents Act, 1988.
A CIP catalogue record for this book is available from the British Library
ISBN 1 86039 657 7 (pb)
Printed in Great Britain by
The Guernsey Press Co. Ltd., Guernsey, Channel Islands

To my friends John, Anamaria,
Alex and John-Paul Ford,
Manuel, Mara, Carlos Andrés,
Manuel de Jesús Alvarez and
Julio Rojas: they have done so much
to further my understanding
of Mexico and its peoples.

PROLOGUE

October 31st. Tijuana, Mexico.

Paco half woke, imagining he had heard the church bell toll twelve times. Luis was coming.

He would kiss the food they had set out for him on the altar. He would play with the toys. He would drink the Coca-Cola.

Paco could almost smell the incense, the beeswax candles, the bread of the dead, the sweet marigolds.

Luis was coming.

Cristina and Maria had scrubbed his gravestone and Paco had carefully filled a piece of chipped stonework. They had all scattered marigolds on the path.

Paco turned over, pulling the blanket over his head.

Sometimes he thought Luis might come as a dove.

As he began to drowse, he heard the song Luis used to sing on Todos Santos:

At six o'clock the skeletons cut their cake,
At seven o'clock the skeletons go to bed,
At eight o'clock the skeletons are asleep.

Luis was coming. Today was the Day of the Dead.

Paco sat up, all traces of sleep thrown aside like the petals of the marigolds rising in the wind. This time Paco wouldn't be here to greet Luis.

How could the spirit of his dead brother ever find his way to California? Without the marigold path?

PART ONE

ONE

October 31st. Mexican Border.

Alex was sure he was going to suffocate.

Crouched in the tiny, pitch-black bucketing space, legs drawn up to his chin, sweat running down his face, handkerchief sodden, head pounding, the panic raged inside him. He wanted to scream and beat at the plastic walls. Instead, he remained petrified by the continuous vibration, the sour smell of his tomb.

How far *was* the border? Could he last out? Even if he could beat at the lid, Alex knew his father wouldn't hear him above the roaring rattle of the noisy diesel engine.

Well, at least the coffin would come in useful. All Dad had to do was bury his bloated, boiled-alive corpse on some scrubby, sage brush blown hillside.

Alex was tall and broad-shouldered, and his knees continually juddered as the coffin shook. Had his father lashed it on tightly enough? Suppose the thing fell off the back of the pick-up and was crushed under the wheels of one of the huge American trucks, with their stove-pipe exhausts and blunt, deep-throated klaxons, hungry monsters of the Californian freeways?

He tried to focus his mind on the Pacific, seeing the powerful clean waves crashing on to the smooth sandy shores of Coronado, but his predicament overwhelmed any attempts he made at keeping calm.

Instead, he saw his father standing in the hotel room, arms folded, his slight paunch overlapping his belt, long blond hair tied back in a trendy pigtail.

'You're not coming with me. And that's final,' he said. But it hadn't been. Now Alex was deeply regretting his own stupidity. They were heading for the Mexican border and he was being cooked alive like an egg.

His head throbbed, but at least he hadn't got asthma like yesterday afternoon when his chest tightened as an enormous wave buried him. Dragging himself out of the surf, he staggered up the beach. He rummaged desperately through the beach bag's jumbled contents – suntan oil, book, hairbrush, Mum's photograph, dark glasses – turning them all over in mounting anxiety until at last he found his Ventolin spray, carefully wrapped in a towel.

As he pumped in the vapour, the frantic wheezing

began to lessen and his shoulders stopped heaving.

'That was nasty.' His father stood over him, looking like a plump walrus in his wetsuit, hair sparkling with droplets of water. If only he wasn't so overweight, he'd look good, Alex thought, and then the other "if onlys" clamoured for attention as they always did. If only he wasn't a stranger. If only he spent more time at home. If only he and Mum could live together without so many rows. If only...

'I know another boy with asthma.' Dad sat down on the sand beside him. 'He's got a Ventolin spray too. Trouble is, he lives in such a polluted place the spray doesn't work – at least, not for long.'

Alex guessed that this boy was Mexican and something to do with his father's latest commission – a photographic essay for a glossy magazine. He had waited hopefully for more information, but was disappointed.

'You all right now?'

'I'm OK, Dad.'

'Don't *call* me that,' his father had said with a burst of irritation. 'I want you to call me Steve.'

Alex nodded reluctantly.

'We need to get to know each other all over again.'

That was certainly true. He reckoned his father must have spent years away from home, continued absences that had made Alex mourn for him almost as if he had died.

But instead of one death there had been many, for

directly his father had arrived home, he was preparing to go off again, leaving presents and money in his wake.

Now, uniquely, Steve, as he was apparently required to call his father, had asked Alex to come out to California where they would have "a great time".

Alex had been very nervous about having a great time and had only reluctantly agreed. America had seemed like a threat. His father more so.

Then this new Steve betrayed him on the very first day of the holiday.

'I've got to go across the Mexican border early tomorrow. He spoke too casually. 'I'll be back the following afternoon. I'm sorry I can't take you. Something's come up. Something to do with work.' He paused, losing eye contact, and Alex stared at him. Was this the "great time" they were meant to be having? How typical. To walk out on him in England was a habit. Out here – it just wasn't possible, and that was the reason Alex, always controlled in his reactions, surprised himself by going into the attack.

'You won't *come* back, will you?'

'Of course I will. It's just that my assignment's been brought forward and there's nothing I can do. I can't afford to pass up the money.'

'Mum wouldn't want you to treat me like this.' Alex could have kicked himself for sounding so pathetically childish.

'She's always been too protective.' His father pounced on the opportunity and Alex felt he had betrayed his mother.

'I'm not staying here on my own.'

'You'll be looked after. I've spoken to the manager. You can have room service all the time – or go to the burger bar.'

Alex was unconvinced. He had been overwhelmed by the hotel, acutely aware that his father didn't fit in. Steve looked too travel-stained, too scruffy for the plush lounges and immaculate tennis courts, the sun-decks full of the rich and famous.

Ever since his father had picked him up from the airport in San Diego, he had felt self-conscious, unable to see how he could "cosy up with him", as Mum had said. 'That's what he wants – just for a while anyway – so it's up to you, Alex.' She had never said, "It's up to you, Alex," before and the bleak statement had made him feel uneasy.

Now, as he bounced up and down helplessly in the sweltering darkness of the plastic coffin, his panic mounted. He had felt fear and anxiety before but never like this.

Minor outbreaks usually began on the games field, where Alex knew he would make a fool of himself because he was no good at sport. It hadn't helped that his father had always excelled at sport, a first-class rugby player, a champion swimmer, capped by the county at cricket.

The fact that he had also made such a success of his work – and that his photographs had recently been included in an exhibition at the Festival Hall on London's South Bank – had only alienated Alex still further. It was bad enough never to see his father, but to have other people praise him was even worse. It made him and Mum feel inferior, as if they were nothing, and now the opportunity had come to share in his father's success, he was sure he had thrown it away.

Suddenly the juddering got worse and Alex's fear became uncontrollable. He felt the vomit rising and swallowed, almost retching, realising the pick-up must have left the freeway for a rutted track.

With his throat dry and parched, Alex felt the first signs of the asthma he dreaded, shortness of breath and a slight wheeze. Surely the dreadful journey would soon come to an end? With a super-human effort he wrenched his mind away from the horror of it all; the experience would at least be something to tell his friends. But would they ever believe him? He could hear himself now: 'I went over the Mexican border in a plastic coffin – no, I really did.'

Last night, refusing to speak to his father yet conscious that his mega-sulk wouldn't stop Steve going, Alex had gloomily watched the Pacific rolling up the sand from his bedroom window. If he had behaved like this with Mum, he knew that she would have come round, but Steve obviously had no such intention. The unfairness brought humiliating tears to his eyes.

His father's absence promised to be as painful as all the others in the past: Christmas, birthdays, virtually all the parents' evenings at school. On the rare occasions he *had* been at home, life was always difficult, with both his parents expecting Alex to pretend everything was all right: expensive outings and presents, frantic jokes, exhausting laughter, "compulsory" enjoyment, his mother's acceptance, her initial refusal to criticise. He had seen her "making do" and "ploughing on", "getting through" until the hard anger Alex felt was like a knot in his stomach.

More recently, however, Mum *had* begun to be critical and that had been harder to bear than when she had tried to pretend that nothing was wrong.

Then the unexpected invitation had come.

Alex still had the letter which had been opened and folded up so many times that it had almost come apart. Last night he had dragged it out of his pocket, reading it yet again for clues.

My dear Alex,

You're growing up and I'm missing it all. We seem to have got like strangers and it's over six months since I've seen you.

I'm sorry my job takes me away so much.

At the moment I'm working in Mexico, setting up a shoot for Atlas magazine which I reckon is my most exciting yet and not nearly as dangerous as all that stuff in Bosnia. What's more, Atlas are going to pay me a bomb if I can bring it off. It's all top secret right now and if anyone finds out what I'm trying to do then there'll be hell to pay.

I'm not sure when I'm going to have to do the shoot, but why don't you come over in the autumn? Say October/November for a couple of weeks. I'm sure you won't mind missing a bit of school!

Where I'm living in Tijuana, one of the Mexican border towns, it's a bit of a dump, so I suggest I treat you to a posh hotel in California, as well as the flights. We could have a good time together and I can get a short holiday.

Do come. I miss you a lot and we could get to know each other all over again, more like friends than father and son. If you know what I mean.

Actually I'm in need of a friend.

Write soon and tell me you're coming. I've sent a separate letter to Mum with all the details.

Your loving Dad –
but why not call me Steve when you come out?
P.S. We'll have a great time!

Letters were all very well, Alex had thought last night, putting it back in his pocket.

But this time his father was in for a shock. He wouldn't meekly accept being deserted. If his father wanted him – *really* wanted him – then he would have to prove it.

All Alex's life, he had felt a lack of purpose. Mum felt much the same and he knew they tended to undermine each other, to shelter in the world they had created, cosy, but a fortified castle they had built against being hurt.

Now, for the first time in his life, he had been angry enough to challenge his father, but when he had spotted the plastic coffins in the back of the truck that evening he had been amazed. Where had they come from? They certainly hadn't been around earlier.

Then Alex remembered that his father had driven into San Diego just before lunch while he had had a rest, still suffering from jet-lag. Had he picked them up then?

Each coffin was painted black and decorated with a line of dancing skeletons, bony hands linked, dark cavities of mouths opened as if in song.

Were they props for this mysterious shoot his father wouldn't talk about?

Suddenly, a mad, impossible, revengeful idea had come to Alex. Suppose he hid in one of those coffins? If he could get inside one, later – much later – he could get out and confront his father. It would serve him right. It would mess up his plans. It would remind this "Steve" that Alex was a person too, someone who could not be dumped as easily as all that.

Then he had remembered something vital. If his father *was* driving across the border wouldn't he need his own passport?

Alex felt triumphant at his planning. But he was also afraid and his fear was increasing every moment.

Next morning, after a restless and troubled night, Alex almost lost his nerve. But not quite. His anger still pushed him on and the incredible plan became a reality.

He left a note under his father's door, explaining that he had gone out for a long walk on the beach and was looking forward to his return the following afternoon. Then he took the lift down to the hotel foyer, hoping against hope that he hadn't left his madcap plan too late.

Alex hurried into the car park and looked around, hesitating, telling himself to go back to bed, to stop acting out of character. Alex Carson didn't stow away in the back of trucks. He was a cautious boy who lived with his mother in Winchelsea. Alex Carson was nervous, retiring. He didn't have that many friends. He'd never had a girlfriend. He didn't like the dark. He was afraid of spiders, being left alone, high winds, strangers, exams, being late, being stupid and not being able to breathe. Alex Carson didn't have adventures.

But the anger had been running hot inside him and he

had been driven by an instinct he had never felt before.

Suddenly, without further thought, Alex ran towards the truck, pulled open one of the coffins, scrambled in and after a good deal of panicky scrabbling closed the lid again.

Once on the road the heat in the coffin had begun to build up, soon becoming unbearable.

Alex had used his Ventolin spray repeatedly, realising that he was overdosing himself but at least able to ease the tightness in his chest, the wheezing, the mounting struggle to breathe. The sweat had run into his eyes while cramp spread in his legs, the pain creeping up to his knees. His feet seemed to have swollen, and his trainers had felt unbearably tight.

Hysteria swept him, making his throat constrict as he fought for control, despite the fact that for the moment his asthma seemed to have retreated. The shiny plastic walls seemed to move in towards him like wet blubbery flesh and he began to scream.

The truck came to a rattling halt and Alex froze, the scream dying in his throat.

The engine ticked over for a while and was then shut off. An ominous silence followed. Had his father heard him, or was he going to start driving again?

Alex lay there, unable to move or speak. He tried to call out but no sound came. It was as if he had suddenly died and his body was a useless shell. But his spirit was still trapped inside.

TWO

Alex could hear his father jumping into the back of the truck, pausing for a moment, then pulling at the lids of the coffins, trying to find out where the scream had come from.

Blessed fresh air flooded the sweaty, stinking space and Alex blinked up into the hard morning light, seeing a red blob of a sun, hearing the buzz of insects. It was like rising from the dead and catching the first glimpse of heaven. Then his father's features swam hazily into view, almost comically twisted in shock. He didn't look much like God.

What have I done, wondered Alex.

Alex began to vomit and wheeze at the same time as he tried to lever himself upright. Slowly he managed to crawl out of the coffin, almost falling, clutching at the slippery sides and jumping stiffly to the ground. Then he began to retch again.

'You're not going to leave me behind. Did you *hear*

that? You're not going to leave me. Not ever again.'

Steve cleaned him up with a towel and a whole packet of wipes, using water from a coolbox. Alex drank the remainder, ecstatic as the cold liquid soothed his dehydrated throat.

'More...'

'OK.' Now this Steve was his servant, bringing him a bottle of warmer water that still tasted like nectar. He drank half of it at a gulp, not wanting to stop.

'You could have suffocated.' His father spoke for the first time. The plastic coffins glinted sinisterly in the harsh sunlight.

How did I survive in there, Alex wondered. Then he reminded himself that he almost hadn't. He had put himself at the most enormous risk and had almost suffocated. But he had survived. It was like being born again. It also gave him a feeling of heady power.

The truck was parked on a dirt road that rose towards brown foothills, small boulders punctuating the scrubby bushes and chaparral. It was very hot. A small lizard was watching them from a brown rock, head cocked slightly to one side, utterly still on the shadowless track.

'You're not taking me back.' Alex started to wheeze again and had to use the inhaler.

There was no reply.

'Did you hear?'

Alex's feeling of power increased. He had never spoken to his father like this before and he realised he was enjoying the experience, paying him back like the day he retaliated when an older boy tried to bully him at school. He had thumped the boy hard several times and watched his enemy retreat in tears. Now Steve was his enemy.

'Haven't you got anything that'll get rid of this smell of sick?' Alex demanded.

His father went to the cabin of the pick-up, re-emerging with an aerosol can of deodorant. 'Shall I spray or will you?' He grinned weakly.

Grabbing the can Alex sprayed himself liberally. Conscious of looking ludicrous he then threw the can on the ground. 'Pick it up,' he ordered.

But Steve wasn't listening. Instead, he was dragging a small camera from a pocket in his belt, and before Alex could react he had taken a couple of shots.

It was like an immediate invasion of his privacy – as if by photographing him, Steve had cunningly got himself inside Alex's innermost being, stripping him of the power he had built up. The camera had always been his father's weapon and Alex knew that unless his ordeal was to be wasted he had to fight back.

'What did you do that for?'

'I've never seen you in a mood like this before. I wanted to put it on record.'

An immense surge of rage consumed Alex. Was he being mocked? Teased? Put down? 'How can you know about my moods? You're always pushing off, aren't you? Leaving me and Mum alone.' To his satisfaction he could see he had scored.

'You've never shown the slightest interest in my career, have you? Either of you.'

'We never see you.'

'Do you think that's what *I* want?'

'Yes,' yelled Alex. 'Of course it is. You don't want us! You've never wanted us. We hardly saw you at all last year.'

'I was in Bosnia, for God's sake. I could have been blown to pieces.'

'You didn't have to go there.'

'It's my *job*. Don't you understand?'

'You could have got another one. Stayed at home, like other fathers.'

'Just an ordinary dad. Is that what you want?'

'You invited me out here so you could show off, didn't you? Mr Big with his stupid cameras. Who *do* you think you are?' Alex suddenly ran at him, clenching his fists. 'I hate you. Don't you know that? Mum hates you too.'

His father quickly shoved his camera back into his belt, but he was caught off guard and Alex head-butted him in the stomach with such force that Steve fell to the stony ground, legs flailing. Alex threw himself on top, pummelling at his father's face. It was years since they had had any physical contact. Now Alex had broken the taboo by behaving like an animal. Triumphantly, he looked down at Steve's face, at the blood on his lips, the incredulity in his eyes. Red-faced, Alex slowly got up, spluttering and gasping in the heat.

Steve struggled to his feet and father and son outfaced each other. There was nothing to say. Then the sound of an engine cutting across the air broke the long, painful silence.

A battered Ford truck rasped and rattled down the dirt track towards them. The ancient vehicle came to a dusty grinding halt and a teenager got out. He was small, dark skinned, with a baseball cap, denim jacket, jeans and cowboy boots.

'You'd better give me a hand with those coffins,' Steve said brightly and artificially. He looked shaken. 'Jaime's come to collect them.'

As Alex helped unload, he asked, 'What are you doing with these then? Are they part of your shoot?' His voice seemed deeper, more aggressive. What had really happened to him in his plastic trap? Had he changed so much?

'They're for a carnival.' Steve appeared hesitant, unsure of himself.

The coffins lay on the ground, their shiny metal handles glinting in the bright sunlight, the dancing skeletons covered in a light patina of dust.

Jaime stepped forward.

'It's this one,' said Steve. 'No need to open it now.' Hurriedly he repeated the phrase in Spanish, as if he had spoken in English by mistake.

Jaime gazed down at the coffin intently. Then he slid off the lid and fumbled inside, easing out a number of thin plastic bags. As he checked them carefully, Alex saw to his amazement that one was filled with dollar bills and the rest with documents.

He watched as Jaime resealed the bags. What was his father doing? Smuggling dollars into Mexico? And what about the rest of the stuff?

'OK. Let's give him a hand.'

They carried the coffins over to the other truck and lashed them down. Alex could hardly believe what was happening.

When they had finished Jaime climbed back into his cab and drove away without looking back, black fumes belching from the exhaust.

'What's the money for?' demanded Alex. 'And those documents?'

'I'll tell you later.'

'Who was Jaime?'

'A kind of go-between. There's no time to talk now. I've got an appointment in Tijuana.'

'Where's that?'

'Just over the border. You'll have to sit in a café for a few minutes. I shan't be long.'

'Are you going to try and get rid of me again?' A wave of panic overtook Alex and the dun-coloured scrub hills seemed increasingly hostile.

'Of course I'm not. But first we've got a problem to sort out. I need to hide the truck.'

Wondering why but not daring to ask, Alex glanced round and then caught sight of what looked like a shed, almost overgrown by bushes and screened by a large cactus. 'What about over there?'

'Check it out. Use your initiative. That's what I have to do all the time. Live on my wits. You and that mother of yours — you've got no idea.' Steve's voice suddenly rose and for a moment Alex thought he was going to lose control, just as he himself had. If they fought, who would win, he wondered. He remembered how he had flattened his father to the ground, and shuddered. The idea of fighting with him again was so repulsive that he couldn't bear to think of the reality of it.

'I'll take a look.'

'Do that.'

Alex pushed through the scrub, scratching himself on a cactus, exclaiming at the pain, but as he got nearer he saw he'd been right; the old lean-to, made of galvanised iron, was huddled against the wall of a long-ruined house.

'It's OK,' he shouted triumphantly.

'Keep your voice down.'

Alex waited, listening to the revving engine, wondering what his father had got mixed up in. Carnival coffins, dollar bills and documents? A go-between? No wonder Steve hadn't wanted to bring him along.

THREE

When they had finished camouflaging the truck with scrub, his father glanced at his watch.

'We're not far from the border. I'll have to get a move on.' He sounded worried.

Alex's reaction was renewed anxiety. 'You're not thinking of giving me the slip? Stranding me out here? You're going to dump me, aren't you?' His voice was sharp with suspicion.

Then to Alex's amazement, his father suddenly threw his arms around him, hugging him tightly, kissing him and muttering, 'Ali – I'm so sorry, Ali.'

He went rigid. His father hadn't called him that since he was about five. Now the pent-up emotion seemed to threaten Alex, closing in like the plastic coffin.

Steve sensed his unease and let go of him. He began to describe Tijuana, his words tumbling over each other, as if he were trying not to let a silence develop.

They walked awkwardly back along the stony track, the sun beating down on them relentlessly.

Ten minutes later they emerged at the border between America and Mexico with its twenty-four traffic lanes split between east and west. As they headed towards the Customs buildings, Steve continued his monologue. 'Tourists are bussed in here to bet on a horse or go to a bull fight or shop or bargain for goods or disco all night. But for Mexicans it's different. They're trapped here, most of them struggling to survive, or make enough money to cross the border. Illegally.'

There was a note of excitement in Steve's voice that was almost infectious. Back in England, Alex had dreamt of adventures, and now he was sharing one with his father. Hadn't he been wanting this all his life? But he kept thinking about the plastic coffins and the hidden money and Jaime the go-between.

'A lot of Mexicans work in factories built by the Americans who rip off the cheap labour, but at least they provide health schemes. Poverty here is worse than you could ever imagine. If you can't get a job then you have to try and sell in the street, or shine shoes or, if you're at the very bottom of the heap, scavenge the rubbish on the dumps.'

'Why don't you come clean, Dad?' Alex was suddenly impatient. 'Tell me what's *really* going on.'

'I told you to call me Steve.'

'Tell me what's *really* going on, Steve.'

'We haven't got time for the whole story. Not now.' He paused. 'We'll go through Customs and – wait a minute! You haven't got a passport.' Steve was horrified, caught out and clearly unable to cope.

'But I have.' Alex was triumphant, delighted he could surprise his father, the sense of his own power returning. 'I knew I had to bring it. Do you reckon I'm stupid or something?'

'Good thinking.' Steve put his arm round Alex's shoulders in attempted affection, but this time he was stiff and awkward. 'You're more resourceful than I thought.'

'What did you think I was like, then? Back in England?' He hardly dared ask the question in case he got the truth.

'I thought you were one hell of a guy.' His father took his arm away.

In the centre of Tijuana, Indian children tried to sell them packets of chewing gum, sombrero hats and cheap toys, while an old woman sat on the pavement, beads and crosses and dolls spread out in front of her.

Alex tried to ignore the children's knowing eyes, guessing they instinctively recognised him as a soft touch. The contrast between this squalor and the smooth lawns and picket fences of California such a short distance away was shattering, and the filthy streets, the stink of exhaust fumes and rotting refuse made him feel sick again.

Up in the surrounding hills, Alex could see shanty housing clinging to the sides of the canyons, poised above the broken tarmac of the roads where the traffic crawled between decaying buildings.

Small bands roved the streets with trumpets and guitars, momentarily drowning the cathedral bell which tolled amid the ceaseless blaring of car horns and the grinding roar of beat-up buses.

On l'Avenida Revolución, shopkeepers in the doorways of their tawdry souvenir shops and bars tried to catch Alex's eye, making him feel embarrassed and awkward, not knowing how to avoid their attentions.

A boy in a skeleton body stocking selling sugar skulls on a tray brushed past them.

'What's he got up like that for?' asked Alex.

'It's the Day of the Dead. Kids dress in that kind of spooky gear and there's celebrations – feasts and music – in the cemeteries. Some families keep their windows open so the souls of dead children can come in for their favourite food. *That's* another reason why I've grown to love Mexico.'

Alex didn't reply, for it seemed to him that Mexico was just another escape route for his father. Yet another rival to Mum.

As they toiled up the steep, litter-strewn hill he saw children selling candy skulls, and a cemetery full of awnings under which offerings of food were being set out. Candles were waiting to be lit, flowers were everywhere and families were already gathering around the graves while small bands played their raucous melodies.

More children ran in and out of the traffic – a continuous stream of ancient buses, fume-belching trucks and battered cars – as they offered their candles and sugar skulls. There were ceramic trees of life in the shops, and a procession of people dressed in more skeleton body stockings slowly crossed the road, provoking a cacophony of hooting.

Suddenly another, even more menacing group appeared: a bride and groom with skeleton heads, escorted by children wearing weeping masks and older boys with chalk-white painted faces.

Stopping in the merciful shade of a pavement café, Alex and his father sipped iced lemonade, silently watching the macabre scene.

'Señor Carson?' A man hovered in the doorway, stick thin with a nugget of a face, wearing a tattered suit. 'There is someone to speak with you.'

Steve got up and winked at Alex. 'I'll be back in five minutes. Order yourself another drink. All the waiters speak English.'

He followed the man into the dark shadows at the back of the café.

Alex drank some lemonade, feeling self-conscious on his own, his anxiety mounting. An American couple were sitting at the next table, talking in low voices and sometimes darting glances in his direction. Next to him was a group of Japanese tourists and a little further down a young woman, also on her own, was reading a book.

His father had been telling the truth for once. There *was* something magical about Mexico. Black magical. Suppose he was abducted from his table by someone in a skeleton body stocking? Suppose he was imprisoned in one of the dark, derelict-looking buildings around him? The alien place closed in on Alex as he watched the dense crowds in the alleyways and side streets that the tourists seemed afraid to enter. Well – he was afraid too. But what of? Steve? Mexico? Or was he just missing his mother?

As a young child, in the days when Dad was at home more, Alex had once got lost on a crowded beach in England. He had wandered off and when he had tried to find his parents again the serried ranks of deckchair sitters had all looked the same, as if they were wearing masks. He had run frantically from chair to chair, trying to identify his parents and becoming increasingly afraid.

Then a figure had swooped down on him and Alex had bawled his lungs out and struck out with his fists.

Until he had realised he was in his father's arms.

Now his eyes combed the upper storeys opposite the café. A youngster was leaning over a rusty iron balcony, watching him intently, holding a canary in a cage. The boy took the bird out and let it settle on his arm, gazing up at the smoky grey sky that was now only slightly flecked with blue. The bright yellow bird made no attempt to fly away and, pushing it back into its prison, the boy turned his back on Alex.

Alex dropped his gaze to a bakery on the opposite side of the street. The window had a huge sign saying *"pan de muerto"* and was full of piled-up bread with skulls traced on the loaves. Could the words mean bread of the dead? There was also a line of sugar skeletons, some dancing as they had done on the plastic coffins.

Alex felt his chest tighten and he took a few puffs from his Ventolin spray. Then he felt easier.

Glancing back at the street, Alex saw a young girl pushing a cart loaded with more bread. Each skull had a name attached to it – Luisa, Paola, Georgina, Jaime. Confectionery hair grew from the heads of sugary ghouls and marzipan corpses lay in chocolate coffins.

A feeling of intense homesickness for the seawashed shingle and silent marshland of Winchelsea swept over him and Alex again wondered why his father never stayed there for long.

Was it because he and Mum were so boring?

37

Compared with Tijuana, Winchelsea must seem very dull. Only the sea was unpredictable, sometimes a glorious blue, streaked with green, but often a sullen grey, lashing itself into a vicious storm and angrily pounding the pebbles, quite different from the majestic Pacific rollers which were friendly and warm and inviting to ride.

'Of course the weather's wonderful out there in California. It makes *all* the difference,' he could hear his mother say, and felt a rush of love for all the security she represented.

'Naturally *he* loves it out there.' Mum rarely used his father's name nowadays. '*He's* having the whale of a time.'

Alex remembered walking along the dykes by the English Channel with the father he had never for one moment thought of as Steve. It had been a stormy morning and he had felt a new excitement as they sat in an old stone shelter and watched the spume and the racing gulls.

They had drunk tea from a flask laced with a little whisky, making him feel heady and warm. As they walked back, his father had asked him not to tell Mum about the whisky. 'She wouldn't understand,' he said. Alex felt torn; relishing doing what his father did, yet worried at having to conceal anything from his mother.

The homesickness deepened still further and tears

pricked at the back of his eyes. Alex saw his mother walking over the pot-holes in the crowded Tijuana street, shaking her head over a dilapidated bus and the stink of its exhaust. 'This just *isn't* good enough,' she said as she advanced on him, wearing her old mac. Her face was pinched and worn and white, and then she vanished down an alley.

Alex finished the last of his lemonade and glanced at his watch. His father had only been gone for a couple of minutes, but already it seemed like an eternity. He stared into the bottom of his glass and then out at the crowded pavements again.

A grinning Indian girl of about his own age was approaching with a tray of candy skulls hanging from a string around her neck. At first Alex tried to ignore her, but she wouldn't go away, determined to make a sale.

She moved nearer, with a smile that looked as if it was painted on her face, and when he tried to wave her away she stayed exactly where she was. He didn't know what to do; he had no money and couldn't speak a word of Spanish. Her eyes were on his and he felt his face reddening, the flush creeping down his neck.

In the end the waiter spoke to her sharply and she disappeared into the crowd, searching for another victim. The waiter grinned at him and then at the American couple as if to say, 'What an idiot this English boy is.'

Again Alex glanced at his watch; just over five minutes had crawled past. He tried not to make eye contact with anyone, staring down at his empty glass, wondering if the waiter might ask him to move on, too inhibited to ask for another drink. If only he had a book. Feeling as if he was being watched by dozens of contemptuous eyes, Alex found himself examining minutely the scarred and stained surface of the plastic table.

A band paused outside the café for a few moments, the music menacingly loud, and a boy in a skeleton mask brushed past him and ran into the dark interior. Firecrackers went off nearby.

The home-made trolley was propelled by a claw-like hand, and at first Alex could hardly believe what he was seeing. He felt incredibly hot and his mouth went dry, but however hard he tried he couldn't turn away. The man had no legs. He was simply a head, torso and two stunted arms at the end of which long talons clasped a begging bowl.

Slowly, more relentlessly than the little Indian girl, he came towards Alex, fixing his eyes on him, demanding, insisting. His waist was bound with soiled cloth and the unoiled trolley wheels squeaked.

With a supreme effort of will, Alex forced himself to his feet and stumbled out of the sunlight into the dark of the cold musty café, searching for the toilets. Steve was nowhere to be seen at the back of the café so Alex ran out into the sunlight again. The legless man had rolled his trolley away, but the waiter was hovering instead.

'You want another drink?'

'My father will pay. When he comes back.'

'OK.' The waiter pointed at his glass. 'What is it?'

'Lemonade. Please. Thanks.'

He returned in a few moments with a fresh drink filled with clinking ice and Alex almost wept with gratitude. At last he had something to do with his hands.

He gazed down at his watch yet again. Twelve minutes. Or was it more? Please come back, Steve, he prayed. Please.

He drank the lemonade slowly, but it was too cold, with a sour taste that threatened to make him choke. Had he been abandoned again? Panic swept him. What could he do?

'All right, old son?' His father's shadow loomed over him, blocking out the sun, just as it had after Alex had been lost on the beach. His relief was incredible. So was his anger.

'Where the hell have you been?'

'I told you I—'

But Alex didn't let him finish. 'Look at the time.'

'I've only been gone a quarter of an hour.'

'You said five minutes!'

'It took a bit longer—'

'You tried to dump me. Again.'

This time the American couple were looking at them both with increasing interest, the Japanese stopped talking and even the young woman glanced up curiously from her book.

Alex cursed himself for being a fool as they walked silently and with mutual hostility through the crowds. He knew he had mishandled the situation, knew that once again he had shown himself up to be childish.

Outside the cathedral there were stalls selling rosaries, prayer cards and candles. Steve hesitated and then to Alex's surprise bought a large candle in a glass jar.

'Let's go inside,' he said.

Tijuana cathedral was very different from St Mark's at Hastings, with its dull priest, small congregation and pale, everyday, commonsense Christianity.

It was impossible to tell exactly *what* people believed here, but their need for faith seemed overwhelming. Had his father picked up that need too?

Although there was no mass being held, the cathedral was almost full, and an old man chanted while Steve Carson lit his candle, placing it below the statue of the Virgin Mary. He didn't kneel, nor did his lips move in prayer.

'I'm sorry,' he muttered as they went to sit in one of the battered pews.

Alex didn't respond for the apology seemed totally meaningless.

'Do you believe in God?' he asked eventually.

'I don't know.'

'Do you pray?'

'Not a lot.'

There was another long silence, finally broken by Alex.

'Where are we going?'

'Out of town.'

'Are you going to tell me why?'

'That's why I brought you here. So we could talk.' He paused. 'I have to go back across the border tonight.'

'I thought that's what we were doing anyway.' Alex was confused, but the fear was back, churning in his stomach.

'I have to get some people across, and not the conventional way either I'm afraid.'

'Why? Who?'

'A family I've got to know.' He paused. 'It's going to make a terrific story. This could be the big one for me.'

His father's voice, almost a whisper, seemed to be booming in Alex's ears, as if he was listening to waves on a shore. A family? *Another* family? Was he involved with them in some way?

'*We're* your family. Mum and I.'

'Of course you are.'

'So what are you on about then?'

A feeling of wild desperation crept over Alex, coupled with a sense of imminent danger, as if the lid of the plastic coffin was closing over him again.

'I was going to explain.' Steve was gazing ahead at the statue of the Virgin Mary.

'So you're going to leave me for good this time?' Alex's fear of rejection went into overdrive. Somehow he forced out the words, his heart pounding so hard that it hurt.

'Of course not,' said his father, wilfully misunderstanding him. 'You're coming across the border with us.'

Alex felt confused. Intuition told him his father was deeply involved with this family, yet perhaps he was wrong to see a threat there.

Then Steve went on: 'I've met a Mexican woman. Cristina. I'm very fond of her.'

'What?' Now Alex felt his worst fears confirmed. Who was this Steve? Certainly not the father he had come all this way to be with.

'I'm helping to smuggle her and her family across the border tonight. I've managed to get hold of a coyote. That means a guide. Well, two of them to be precise. They seem to work as a partnership. They're also grossly expensive, they call the tune about the timing of the crossing and suddenly I was told tonight's the night. You have to use coyotes even over so short a distance. The mountains are full of gangs just waiting to beat up and rob people who are trying to cross.' Steve paused.

'Anyway – I've carefully checked out these coyotes and I know they're genuine. Naturally they've already asked for more money, and I knew I could be searched at Customs. So they hit on the coffins. They're used in carnival processions and we were all sure they wouldn't arouse any suspicion. Jaime's job was to drive them across the border.'

'Who else is in this family?' Alex asked, the shockwaves hammering at him.

'Paco and Maria – Cristina's kids. They're going to work on a fruit farm.' He paused. 'She had another child. Luis. But he died.'

'They won't have any papers.'

'There won't be any questions asked.'

Alex's mind reeled. 'What about Mum?'

'That's over.'

'Are you going to stay out here?'

'I don't know. I might. I'd have to get a work permit if I did.'

The bleakness spread inside Alex, but his father was strangely calm.

'You're coming across the border with us. Then I'll stay on at the Del till you fly home. Cristina's son – Paco – he gets asthma like you, but worse. The pollution's really bad here. He could die if he doesn't get to California.

Like his brother Luis.' Steve paused. 'I wouldn't say that working conditions for illegal immigrants are much better in the US – and the rates of pay are lousy. But, to Cristina, California's like a new beginning. Particularly for Paco. I'm certain his asthma's going to ease off if I can get them across.'

The old man was still chanting and someone else had started praying aloud a few pews away.

Alex didn't want to think about this family. He only wanted to concentrate on his own.

'What are you going to tell Mum?'

'I don't know. Yet.'

Alex couldn't take it all in. His mind kept going off at a tangent.

'Those coffins,' he blurted out. 'Where did you get them from?'

His father was silent.

'Well?'

'The coyotes have another business interest.'

The more questions Alex asked, the more open Steve seemed to become. It was like peeling off the skins of an onion.

'What is it?'

'Forged papers – passports and visas. They ordered a coffin with hidden compartments.'

'You could have been caught. And jailed.'

'I wasn't driving them over the border. Jaime was.'

'Who made you do this?'

'*Made* me? I make my own decisions, thank you.' Steve seemed offended.

'Did you make a decision to leave Mum?'

'Of course I did. We don't have anything in common any more.'

'She loves you.'

'She had a funny way of showing it.'

'You always pushed off.'

'I have to work.'

It was hopeless. The conversation was circular. We could sit here for hours, thought Alex, and still never get anywhere.

The enormity of what his father intended to do swept over him and he saw Mum sitting bolt upright a few pews away. Despite the heat she was wearing a headscarf and eating the Marmite sandwiches she always made when they went for walks.

'You can't leave us,' Alex whispered. 'You can't.'

'But I already have.'

FOUR

Outside the cathedral a dark carnival of a procession passed them, headed by musicians with drums and trumpets, and followed by a macabre bridal couple. He wore a body stocking painted with bones, boots, a military tunic, a dead white skeleton mask and a cap. She was also dressed in a bony body stocking, but with a red dress and a much more hideous skeleton mask with huge tombstone-like teeth. She also wore a broad black hat decorated with a red plume.

Then there followed a group of dancing, tumbling, gyrating skeletons. Finally some children with death masks pranced along, painted tears running from painted eyes.

The band thumped their drums, blowing raucously on their trumpets, beating time for the dead.

An antiquated bus took Alex and his father further up into the hills, and as it ground painfully on Alex saw yet another cemetery filled with flowers. The graves were ornate and some had toy windmills whirling in the light breeze and glass cases containing toys and photographs of children.

Soon they were passing canyons overspilling with shanty towns. Most of the houses were built of tin, reinforced with old tyres or galvanised iron, but incongruously there were satellite discs on some of the roofs and beat-up cars or trucks were parked outside.

At the top of the hill there was a distant view of the sea. In a valley below, Alex saw more shacks, but this time some were strongly built with breeze blocks and wooden roofs.

'This is where we get off.'

'How much Spanish do you speak?' asked Alex, forgetting to keep up what he hoped was a condemning silence. How *could* he be doing this? Mum would never recover from such a final blow.

'Not a lot. But Cristina's kids go to school and study English. Anyway – all three of them are always trying to perfect the language. They've been dreaming about California for a long time. Too long.' Steve grinned. 'Besides – they watch wall-to-wall soap operas on American TV channels here.'

Despite his father's long absences, despite the fact Alex felt he hardly knew him, the news about Cristina had already made Alex's fragile world fall apart. He felt numb, seeing his mother everywhere, and when he closed his eyes against the misery of it all, he saw her again, only this time she was wearing a weeping death mask.

The shacks were crowded tightly together in the broad, gently sloping canyon. Chickens pecked at the stony ground, music blared from ghetto blasters.

'Why does Cristina live in these conditions?' asked Alex hesitantly.

'Her father's business failed years ago and she had a row with the boss in a bottling plant. She's not an easy person – and recently it's been downhill all the way.'

Piles of refuse were stacked at the top of the hill and a bulldozer was pushing some of it around in the light blue heat haze. The more crudely built shacks leant at crazy angles, with walls made of board and bits of wood from fruit crates, the gaps sealed with plastic sheeting.

Black and white TVs blared, hooked up to ancient car batteries, and tyres filled with dirt and geraniums did service as gardens. Each shack had a fence made from the coils of burnt mattresses, and the surrounding streets had been carved out of baked mud. There was a strong smell of sewage. Alex saw that he was standing on a narrow pathway sprinkled with marigold petals.

'How can anyone live here?'

'They don't have any choice.'

Steve rapped at the half-open door of one of the shacks and a boy of about Alex's age came out, smaller, stockier, gazing at him curiously, his face square with a thatch of black hair. There was something tentative about him, as if he were waiting to be let down, to be disappointed.

'Tonight's the night,' said Steve brightly.

But the doubt remained in the boy's eyes.

'This is Paco. Meet Alex. I hope you'll be good friends...' Steve's voice tailed off as if two separate worlds had suddenly collided.

Alex felt the same. The contrast between the comfortable world of California and the misery of this shanty town could not have been greater.

Reluctantly he followed his father into a small dark space with gaps for windows over which sacks had been hung. A single bulb lit the centre of the room and there were a few pieces of broken furniture, an old stove, a large TV set and a pile of mattresses at the back. There didn't seem to be any other rooms.

Then Alex saw the altar. A trestle table had been pushed back against the far wall and was covered in flowers and coloured silk, dominated by the photograph of a young boy who looked like Paco. Candles flickered in glass jars.

The name LUIS was picked out in paper cut-outs and on the altar table itself were sweets, a toy bus, a bottle of Coke and a couple of small T-shirts still in their shop wrapping.

A slight figure with long, dark hair and a square face

like Paco's emerged from the shadows. Her eyes were sombre and her features set. Was she his mother's rival? If so, Mum didn't stand a chance.

'Who's this?' said the woman suspiciously.

'My son.'

'What's he doing here?' She was angry.

'I can't leave him on his own.'

'You don't mean he's coming with us?'

'I've got no choice.'

'Then you're a fool.'

A man appeared in the doorway behind them and a furious argument broke out in Spanish.

Alex couldn't understand a word of what was being said, but it was obvious that his father was losing. It was equally obvious that his Spanish wasn't very good, judging by how much Steve hesitated and then searched for words.

Eventually the man bellowed in English, 'You bring your son! What kind of idiot are you? Isn't it enough that your magazine is humiliating my sister?'

'They're helping to pay for an expensive crossing.' Steve was trying to assert himself now. 'This is Cristina – and her brother, Manuel.' He couldn't have chosen a worse moment for the introductions and Alex felt a flicker of amusement which quickly faded with the grim realisation that, once again, he could still be left behind. However would he manage on his own in a place like this? Suppose his father never came back and he was trapped here for ever?

'You know it's illegal to cross the border without papers?' demanded Manuel. He gazed menacingly at Alex, wanting to force him into speech and not allow him the role of innocent bystander.

'It's not my father's fault. I hid in the back of his truck.' Alex paused, not wanting to mention the coffins, wondering whether Cristina knew about them or not.

'You disobeyed your father?' she asked.

'I had to.'

She smiled and shrugged, almost as if she approved of his disobedience. Alex had passed some kind of mysterious test.

'He can carry another rucksack,' Steve put in hopefully.

'Paco's asthma is bad here,' Cristina explained, addressing Alex as if he was an adult. 'He needs fresh air, like in California. My sister has written to tell me the farm will let us in – if we can get there. She hasn't got any papers either but her kids are in school.'

Cristina turned to the altar and her eyes filled with tears.

'But of course we shall have to leave Luis behind.'

What *does* she mean, Alex wondered. She was talking as if he were still alive.

There was a long, tense silence which was eventually

filled by Steve. 'Carlos says the crossing may be expensive, but it'll be fast.'

He's so unsure of himself here, thought Alex.

'He's a liar.' Cristina's voice was dismissive.

'I thought you said you trusted him.'

'I don't trust anyone.'

Breaking into the hostilities, Paco suddenly nudged Alex. 'You want to play football?'

He didn't, but anything would be better than the atmosphere inside the shack.

The sky was steel grey. The smell outside seemed even more pungent now, and gulls were hovering above the dump, searching for food.

Where the canyon broadened there was a dirt pitch with goal posts hanging at crazy angles. A number of boys were kicking a ball around.

What are you? A wimp or a wimp? His school PE instructor's voice probed Alex's mind. He didn't see himself as anything of the kind. He liked cross country running, playing squash, canoeing. What he didn't like was team games. "*It's your fault, Carson. You let the team down.*" Gazing round the dirt pitch, Alex's spirits plummeted still further. He felt he was going to let everyone down.

Paco got out an asthma spray at the same time as Alex and they both grinned at each other warily, not sure whether they were pleased to admit they had Ventolin in common.

Then Paco headed off towards the pitch, yelling in Spanish at the other boys, while Alex followed apprehensively.

The pick-up match under the leaden sky was just about as bad as he had expected, with the dust thick and choking and the play fast and rough. But there wasn't any cat-calling or derision, and despite the fact that he got knocked down a couple of times Alex felt unexpected pride at being accepted – until he realised he was probably being ignored.

They've never known anything else. The voice in his head was his mother's. It was as if all the bitterness caused by his father's long absences had made her prejudiced. *They've never known anything else.* But it wasn't fair, Alex thought, as he ran around the ball. Why should anyone have to live this way?

Eventually the game came to an end as if at some unspoken signal. Could it be lunch time, he wondered, his spirits rising. From behind an abandoned cooking stove, Paco produced a bottle of water which was warm and slightly gritty.

Alex took a long swig – he was surprisingly thirsty. Amazingly he wasn't wheezing at all, but Paco was – and badly. As he passed the bottle back to him he saw he was using the spray again.

'I'm no good at football,' admitted Alex.

'So what?'

What about his lack of skill, he wondered uneasily. His crafty avoidance of the ball? Back home he would have been jeered at. But here, it seemed, it was enough to play.

He watched Paco use the spray again but it didn't seem to be doing any good. He leant against the rusty stove, his shoulders heaving, breathing shallow, the wheezing a rasp.

'If you use the spray too much it doesn't work.'

Paco still said nothing, but Alex noticed he was getting calmer, the wheeze decreasing a little.

'In California, it'll be different,' Paco said at last. 'We'll be there tomorrow.' But he looked at Alex doubtfully, as if he still didn't really believe in the idea. 'We were going before. But we never made it.'

Alex couldn't think of anything to say.

'Can you trust Steve?' asked Paco.

Suddenly it seemed essential to be honest. 'I don't know.'

Paco looked disappointed. 'What do you mean?'

'I haven't seen much of him lately. He's always away.'

'Where?'

'Here.' Alex paused. It was as if, for the first time, he could really tell the truth. 'Anyway, he and Mum are going to break up.' Now that he had put the statement into words, Alex felt curiously flat, as if he had used up all possible emotion.

'Break up?'

'Steve might go away.' He didn't want to say any more. How much did Paco know, he wondered. How much had Cristina told him?

'My father. He went away,' Paco said unexpectedly. His breathing seemed better now and the wheezing had almost stopped.

'How come you speak such good English?' asked Alex, awkwardly changing the subject. He didn't want to exchange confidences, even if he had initiated them.

'School.'

Paco's eyes had a foggy look now and Alex guessed that he was angry inside. 'When my mother lost her job we came here. But I still go.'

'What about your sister?'

'She works with my mother on the dump.' Paco was gazing at Alex's watch now. 'That's good.'

'What is?'

'The watch is good.'

Alex unstrapped it. His father had given it to him last Christmas, forgetting he had already bought him one the Christmas before. Alex had been bitterly hurt. Now it didn't matter.

'Take it.'

'What will Steve say?'

'Nothing. Anyway I've got another one at home.'

Paco slid the watch into his pocket with considerable pleasure.

The gift's real, Alex thought. California isn't. Like his father wasn't.

'Why not put it round your wrist?'

Paco said nothing, and took another swig of the water, wiping his mouth with the back of his hand.

'My father – have you known him long?' asked Alex curiously.

Paco shrugged, evasive now.

'He likes your mother.' He felt compelled to angle for information.

'He's rich?' Paco asked with sudden interest, as if the idea had only just occurred to him.

'I don't think so.'

'You are right. He likes my mother.'

'But he hardly knows her.' Alex was now backtracking as fast as he could. He had gone too far.

'Do you want to be my brother?' asked Paco suddenly, watching him closely.

Alex wasn't sure whether he was sending him up or asking a genuine question. It must be his idea of a joke, he thought.

'What?'

'Suppose your father marries my mother?'

'He'd have to get a divorce first,' Alex replied, trying to

laugh it off. In his mind's eye he saw his father and Cristina in an old movie. *I'll take you away from all this*, Steve said as he led her out of the shack and on to a Californian beach with the frothy white waves washing the sand.

Paco grabbed his arm as if he knew the subject needed to be changed. 'You come.'

'Where?'

'To the dump. To see the border. Come with me. Brother.'

Alex winced at the word, but suddenly he wondered if it wasn't meant as a joke after all.

FIVE

Ahead of him, Paco negotiated a narrow, well-worn path through piles of refuse. The smell was terrible and when they crested a rise Alex came to a halt, gazing down at what looked like a land-locked sea. As the breeze rustled plastic bags, newspapers, toilet tissue, streams of computer paper and black rubbish sacks, they made a soft shifting sound like waves breaking on a shore.

Figures scavenged the dump with long poles which ended in hooks made of bent pegs.

'What are they looking for?'

'Bottles, tins, metal, cloth, wood, furniture.' Paco paused. 'Maybe meat that's not too rotten to be cooked.'

Below the scudding rubbish, Alex could see layers of festering muck. A pack of dogs covered in sores and bites snarled and fought over the debris, while on the horizon the skyscrapers of San Diego gleamed gold.

Dust was rising in the wind and he could feel it in the

back of his throat, thick and cloying. No wonder Paco wheezed so much.

A huge truck full of more rubbish lumbered and snorted its way up from a side road, klaxon sounding, while a couple of bright orange tractors rode over the mounds towards it.

Gulls, crows and pigeons repeatedly dived, competing with the dogs who howled in protest and made feeble attempts to chase them off.

Then Alex saw wisps of smoke drifting from a deeper layer of debris.

'It's on fire,' he said.

'There's methane gas too. Like it's a volcano waiting to blow up. There's a church on the other side and a graveyard. It doesn't rain often here, but when it does it comes down hard. The bodies are sometimes washed right out of the ground.' Paco paused and looked away. 'Once my brother's body came up. My mother found him.'

Alex stared at him, horrified at the terrible image that appeared in his mind.

'She wouldn't let us see Luis. They put him back and then the priest came.'

Flies droned and clouds of huge bluebottles hovered over what looked like fencing posts. Paco saw him looking. 'The trucks keep bringing them.'

'What are those things sticking out of the ground?' Alex had a horrible presentiment.

'Dead animals. Dogs, cats, goats, sometimes horses. They get piled up and burnt.'

He shuddered as he gazed at the charred bones standing sentinel in the stinking haze.

'Sometimes, at night, maybe in the winter when it's colder, we look out at San Diego – at the skyscrapers.'

There was a scampering rustling sound and a huge rat, overweight, panting slightly in its effort to move, staggered slowly away from a pile of old clothes and towards the carbonised animals. It probably feasts all day, thought Alex, the nausea welling up inside him. Then, on the edge of the dump, he saw lean-to buildings covered in plastic sheeting. People live here, he thought. Right in the dirt.

The plastic bags stirred again as the wafting, foul-smelling breeze increased.

'We're lucky not to live right on the dump,' said Paco as they walked away.

Alex nodded, not knowing how to reply. Then he saw a dog limping towards them, one ear almost ripped off, a dark, rancid-looking hollow where an eye should have been, lips parted in a snarl.

'Don't touch her.'

'I wasn't going to.'

But she was coming straight for Alex and Paco grabbed a stick. Alex saw the bitch's yellow teeth and black saliva and knew she was horribly diseased.

Paco hit her on the flank with his stick and with a

howl of pain she stopped, her thin hackles rising in defensive anger. Then she whined and ran back to the pack who received her with yapping barks.

'Do you want to see Luis?' he asked.

For a terrible moment Alex thought Paco's brother had been washed out of his grave again. 'What do you—'

'We're not going to see him – not for a long time. My uncle will care for Luis when we're gone. It's hard to leave him.'

Paco was suddenly close to tears.

On the other side of the dump was a small valley. A church lay in the centre, surrounded by elaborate graves, many of which looked more like miniature chapels. Hundreds of candles were ready to be lit and paths of marigolds led up towards the shanty town.

'What are the flowers on the ground for?' asked Alex.

'They are paths to lead the souls of the dead back home.'

'I don't get it.'

'The souls of dead kids come home tonight – when the church bell rings twelve times. We light candles and open the door so Luis can come in. He's got his favourite food and drink and toys laid out – even some new clothes.'

'You mean he's going to eat and drink and...'

'His spirit will kiss the food and then we'll eat it afterwards. Luis will stay the night and then he'll bless the breakfast of chocolate and bread and fruit, but when the bell rings twelve times again, he'll return to his grave.' Paco paused. 'That's why Mother is so sad. She won't be here to keep the vigil. We'll be on the Mesa instead. My uncle and aunt will keep it for us...'

'Couldn't you have gone another day?'

'Your father says it's the only time the coyotes can make the journey. We're not ready. Today is a bad time to go. What's Luis going to do?'

Now they were walking through the tombs to the far side of the graveyard, still following the marigold paths.

Several families were washing headstones when they arrived and Paco greeted them and then knelt down in front of a small but beautifully kept grave. Under his name – LUIS RUIZ – there was the same photograph Alex had seen on the altar.

He stood awkwardly beside Paco, not knowing what to do or say. Was he praying? Did he want to be silent? Then he asked bluntly, 'What are those words underneath his name?'

'It means: May the sacred rosary break your chains.'

Alex wished he hadn't asked. 'I see,' he said lamely, not seeing at all. He looked down at a glass box on the grave. In it were two shelves crowded with model cars.

'He says he doesn't mind staying here. He doesn't mind us going to California.' Paco sounded confident, but Alex thought Luis's forgiveness sounded too convenient.

'If only my mother could hear him.'

'Doesn't she?'

'She won't listen.' Paco looked up at Alex. 'Luis doesn't mind you being my brother either. He says I need one.'

As they walked back up the hill Alex could smell something pungent and aromatic. Turning a corner they came across an old woman burning weeds and bits of wood, debris from the cleared-up graves. She was incredibly wizened and gnarled and as she scrutinised Alex, she made the sign of the cross. Seeing the old woman silhouetted against the skyline, Alex imagined her to be the Angel of Death.

Back at Paco's home, the earlier tension had vanished. Manuel had left and Steve and Cristina were drinking coffee, talking in fractured Spanish with an unsettling intimacy. Alex felt like an intruder as he and Paco ate some tacos.

Then the canvas door was pushed open and a girl appeared, slightly taller and thinner than Paco.

'So *you're* back,' she sneered at Steve.

'I told you we'd probably be going tonight.' Steve sounded defensive.

'I didn't believe you.'

'Carlos and Oscar are fixed up.'

'For the hell of a price.'

'The magazine is paying. This is Maria. The last

member of our expedition. My son Alex.' Once again Steve was making introductions as if he had come across her in Winchelsea High Street. It was oddly touching but also ridiculous.

Maria looked away.

'Father Antonio will be here soon,' said Cristina, intervening quickly. 'He's going to give us a blessing.'

Maria laughed derisively. 'When has he ever brought anyone luck? Last time he blessed Lupita she died a few hours later.'

'He's not meant to bring luck. And you knew Lupita was dying.'

'We'll need luck,' Maria pronounced. 'Not blessings.' She glanced at Alex for the first time. 'What do we want him for? He'll just get in the way.' She paused and then spoke with real bitterness. 'Or has he come to see you work your miracle, Steve? Smuggling Mexican trash over the border.'

'We just played football,' Paco interrupted. 'He's my friend,' he added.

The word brother hovered in the air but wasn't mentioned. Neither did Paco tell his mother that he had taken Alex to his brother's grave.

Cristina and Maria began to pack up the family's belongings in some battered rucksacks while Steve and Paco watched TV and drank beer.

Alex still felt completely out of place with nothing to

do, ill at ease with himself as much as with the others. In the end he asked Cristina if he could help.

'No,' said Paco turning round before his mother had a chance to reply. 'That's women's work. Steve's bought beer.'

'I don't like it.'

'All men like beer.'

'This one doesn't.' Alex was determined to assert himself. However pleased he had been by Paco's show of friendship, he was determined to hang on to his own identity.

'Mexican beer is strong.'

'No thanks.'

'At last.' Maria dumped a bulging rucksack by the canvas door. 'A man who can make up his own mind.'

Alex felt a surge of elation. He was pleased to have the approval. It had been worth sticking up for himself. He glanced across at his father but Steve's eyes were fixed on the television screen.

Eventually Alex dozed off in front of the television, but he was jolted back to life by the sound of screeching brakes.

Paco stood up and Maria moved across to her mother. Little motes of dust spun in a sunbeam as mellow afternoon light filtered the shack.

'That'll be the coyotes,' said his father, artificially eager, as if he was speaking a line in a bad film.

* * *

Carlos was tall and laid back, with cowboy boots, denim jeans and a flowery Hawaiian shirt. His long black hair brushed his shoulders. Oscar was shorter. He wore a pair of old corduroy trousers and a tattered shirt, and his short hair was receding. Alex found him much the more threatening of the two. His smile seemed permanently fixed and there was no telling what was behind it. Were they really guides, he wondered, remembering they also traded in forged papers. Had his father really checked them out properly? Or were they simply a couple of crooks?

Either way, the excitement of the adventure suddenly surged in Alex again. Was he going to have a story to tell! Here was something he shared with Steve. "A chip off the old block," his mother had once told him when Alex was very young and had gone off for a walk on his own. It had taken him a long time to understand what she had meant and even longer to recognise what she had been so afraid of.

'This is my son. He's coming with us.' The fatal words appeared yet again and Alex waited for the explosion. It was not long in coming.

'No he's not,' said Carlos quietly and without hesitation. 'He's not part of the deal.'

'He *has* to come.' Little droplets of sweat glistened on Steve's forehead and Alex was afraid that his father would be unequal to this final battle.

'We make the decisions.' Carlos was adamant.

Paco tried to intervene. '*I* want him to come.'

'You shut your mouth. He stays here. You can come back and pick him up later.' The smile was fixed on Oscar's face.

'No chance.' Steve went to his rucksack and pulled out some dollar bills. 'How much more do you want? You've already cost the magazine a fortune.'

'It's not a question of money. Your son will put us in danger.'

'Why?' intervened Paco again.

'I told you. Shut your mouth.'

Meanwhile Steve was waving the dollar bills in Carlos's face.

'Your son is not part of the deal,' he repeated.

'He is now.'

Carlos turned to Cristina. '*You* want to take another kid?'

She didn't reply.

'There's an English expression.' Steve made a desperate stab at humour. 'In for a penny, in for a pound. Have you heard it?'

'I don't want to hear it.'

'We'll take him.' Maria suddenly spoke and Alex was surprised by her unexpected support.

'It's not your decision,' said Carlos, but he kept gazing

at Steve's dollar bills.

'He's coming with us,' Cristina said with considerable authority. 'If he doesn't, the deal's off.'

Oscar frowned, but Carlos was won over. 'OK. We'll take him. But if anything goes wrong, we'll walk out on you. And then what will happen to the Ruiz family? And your story for the magazine?'

Alex felt a flood of relief now that the final decision had been made. He was also puzzled. Why *should* they want to take him?

Then he thought about his father paying the coyotes – not just for the family but for the story as well. What *were* Steve's real motives?

Maria put salsa music on the battered ghetto blaster, more beer was produced and neighbours began to drop in. For a while Alex once again hovered on the edge of the crowd, not knowing what to do or say. Despite their unexpected support, Maria and Cristina seemed to be ignoring him now, as were his father and Paco.

Alex had the unsettling impression that they were in some other place and time and he was an outsider looking in.

Then Carlos poured him pale golden liquid from a bottle.

The stuff tasted of fiery sunshine and baked herbs.

'What's that you're drinking?' bellowed Steve.

'Tec something I think.'

'Tequila? That's strong. Why don't you stick to beer?'

'I told you, I don't like it.' Alex was already heading back towards Carlos who still had the bottle. 'Any more of that?' he asked, holding out his glass.

'You like tequila?'

'It's great.'

'Come back for more.' He grinned at him. 'It'll make the journey easy.'

'How far are we going?'

'Just over the hills on the border. We'll climb them when it's dark.'

'Why do we have to get across there?'

'It's the safest crossing.'

'Are the hills easy to climb?'

'If you've had a lot of tequila, yes.' Carlos laughed and Alex decided he liked him after all. 'There's a canyon that drops off the Otay Mesa into a snake pit of gulches and trails.'

'Is there much undergrowth?'

'Brush, mesquite and tamarisk. Don't worry. We'll all make it.' Carlos grinned at Alex and he grinned back.

The more Alex drank the more he liked everybody. Then he saw Oscar watching him with his fixed smile; here was one person he *didn't* like.

Gradually the party began to blur and Alex felt increasingly optimistic. Now he knew why his father loved Mexico. It might be poor but it was also friendly. He didn't care what Mum thought.

He had played football and been accepted. Now he was drinking tequila, and soon he was about to embark on the most exciting adventure of his life.

His mother would be furious, but Alex couldn't wait until he had a chance to tell his friends. Would they believe him? He only half believed in the expedition himself.

The room seemed to grow smaller and hotter, and he went outside. Looking up towards the dump in the twilight, he saw an old couple carrying candles up the path to the graveyard.

The semi-darkness had softened the harsh outlines of the shanty town and the glowing lights were almost welcoming.

Alex watched as a young priest came striding up the track. He wore trainers and jeans underneath his cassock and Paco ran up to him. They slapped palms and spoke in Spanish for a while.

Then Father Antonio turned to Alex.

'This is a bad idea. The Otay Mesa is no place for foreigners.' Alex didn't know what to say.

'I've already told your father this but he chooses not to listen. I don't know these coyotes either. They are not from round here. You have to realise you could be robbed. Or worse.'

'He says they were recommended,' said Paco. 'Steve

says we can rely on them.'

'Have you spoken to them?' asked Alex uneasily.

'What good would that do? Especially if they are thieves.' Father Antonio seemed determined to believe the worst.

'You must speak to them, Father,' Paco insisted. 'Can't you do that?'

'It won't do any good.' The young priest seemed very concerned. 'I was told you wouldn't be going for at least another fourteen days. Now it's tonight of all nights.'

Steve was lying on a mattress, asleep and snoring. Alex grabbed his father's shoulder.

'You drunk, Dad?'

'Are you?' His voice was slurred. 'I told you to call me...'

'Father Antonio wanted to make sure that Carlos and Oscar could be trusted.'

Steve yawned and looked impatient. 'Of course they can. I told you – I had them carefully checked out.' He hauled himself up shakily and looked at his watch. 'Almost time to go. Just a walk over the hills. Where's your watch?'

'I gave it to Paco.'

'Was that a good idea?'

'He wanted it.'

'You shouldn't have given in to him.'

Before Steve could ask any more questions, Father Antonio returned, followed by Cristina, Maria and Paco and what seemed like dozens of other well-wishers. Carlos and Oscar were nowhere to be seen, as if they had tactfully withdrawn from an emotional family occasion.

As Alex gazed round the crowded room he couldn't detect any jealousy. Despite the fact that they were condemned to remaining on this stinking dump, none of Cristina or Maria or Paco's friends betrayed any other emotion than pleasure.

Meanwhile, Father Antonio was talking to Steve. Alex didn't have to hear what his father was saying; he knew how he could persuade people. But it didn't look as if he was persuading the priest. Then Steve beckoned to Cristina, who launched into a long explanation, and Alex kept hearing Paco's name.

Eventually Father Antonio shrugged, and a few minutes later he began to speak. The room quietened and he prayed in Spanish. Then he paused and said in English, 'Wherever this salt and water are sprinkled, let it drive away the power of evil, and protect us always by the presence of your Holy Spirit.'

He poured the salt into water in a bowl and called Cristina, Maria, Paco, Steve and Alex into the centre of the room by the table. Father Antonio sprinkled them with the salt and holy water.

Alex felt a curious sense of protection.

Then the priest made the sign of the cross on their foreheads. When he had finished there was applause and glasses were filled up again.

Alex watched his father put his arm around Cristina and kiss her on the lips. He couldn't remember him giving his mother more than a hasty peck. She's so much stronger than Mum, he thought. Was that why Steve was so attracted to her?

Then Manuel arrived and he watched Cristina take him to the altar. She began to cry and he held her close.

A horn blasted impatiently from outside.

'They're ready.' Paco sounded excited but Alex noticed he was clenching and unclenching his fists. He was also beginning to wheeze again. 'My mother wants to go down to Luis's grave but your father says there's no time.'

Cristina, Maria and Paco were hugged and kissed by their neighbours, and as Alex watched he knew he had never seen such a blending of pain and affection. He glanced at his father and for a moment they caught each other's eyes. Was this the kind of love they had both been missing all those years?

In his mind's eye Alex saw his mother watching from the doorway. The dirt, the dump, the music, the drink – there was nothing that she would approve of at all. Mum wouldn't understand. But then Alex thought, perhaps she had never understood what made his father happy.

Carlos shoved the rucksacks into the boot of the old Buick and joined Oscar in the front. Paco squeezed in beside them while Alex and his father sat either side of Cristina and Maria on the bench seat at the back.

Staring out of the window he noticed Father Antonio gazing at Carlos and Oscar with considerable suspicion. The priest looked as if he would have liked to have stopped it all, but had realised he was too late.

Steve Carson picked up his camera but Oscar intervened, the smile for once wiped off his face. 'You don't take our pictures.'

'I'm not.' He turned his camera on the priest. Dust was rising in the air and a couple of chickens squawked their way across the track while the mangy dogs howled from the dump. The crowd outside the shack began to clap as Oscar drove down the canyon, scattering livestock.

Alex looked back at the dump and saw the bulldozer slowly moving across the refuse. Gulls dived, as if they were following a ship.

Beside him, Cristina was crying and he saw her open a small box and scatter a couple of marigold petals out of the window.

It's not much of a path, thought Alex. But maybe it would be enough to guide Luis's spirit to California.

PART TWO

SIX

The night was chilly, the landscape arid, dark chaparral and boulders sharply etched in bright moonlight. Alex gazed out at the rocky hillside of the Otay Mesa, behind which flickered the lights of Tijuana.

Oscar braked sharply and backed the Buick under some withered trees.

He spoke in Spanish and then in English. 'We will cross the border where the fence has been washed away by the rain. That's why we have to move fast. It should take us about four hours.'

Alex felt a little more reassured. Four hours didn't seem long. Maybe the expedition was going to be easier than he had imagined.

As Cristina got out she dropped another petal.

The hills were full of shifting shadows and the track was steep and littered with loose shale. Alex slipped several times but managed to stay on his feet, picking his way carefully, the rucksack heavy on his back, anxious not to let anyone down.

His head still stung from the tequila and his mouth was dry. It seemed a very long time since he had stowed away in his father's truck, but surely nothing, absolutely nothing, could be as bad as suffocating in a plastic coffin.

Carlos and Oscar strode out in front and only Maria hung back, complaining about the beginnings of a blister. Oscar occasionally turned and spoke to her encouragingly, but Alex could sense that he was becoming impatient.

Down below, in Tijuana, a huge firework display was in progress and Alex could dimly hear the strident beat of the bands.

After a couple of hours, Carlos stopped at the bottom of a dark gully which had a deep, rank smell that made Alex choke. 'We wait here till after midnight.'

Rubbish was everywhere, including piles of filthy blankets, rather as if an army had camped here for a long time and then gone into battle.

'What's the hold-up?' rapped Steve, immediately anxious.

'The helicopters have been making regular surveillance checks this week. We need to keep down for a while.'

There was an uneasy silence. What's the point of waiting, wondered Alex. Surely the helicopters flew every night and didn't conveniently take breaks for illegal immigrants to get across the border? Carlos's instructions didn't really make sense.

'Fair enough,' said Steve. 'We're in your hands.'

'The Border Patrol uses OH6 Alpha helicopters,' continued Carlos as if he wanted to assert himself with his professional knowledge and remind them the coyotes were firmly in charge. Did Carlos see a potential rival in Steve? Alex felt flattered on his father's behalf.

'How do they catch people with a helicopter?' demanded Maria. 'Or do they shoot them instead?'

'They're very gentle those gringos,' laughed Oscar. 'They have two pilots. One flies the helicopter. The other aims a bank of quartz halogen lights. They herd illegals down the trails like flying sheepdogs, right into the arms of the Border Patrol in the beat-up Broncos or Chevrolet Blazers.'

'But they won't be doing that to us,' said Steve firmly. 'You're going to look after us too well, aren't you?' There was an edge to his voice. 'Think of the dollars I paid you for the crossing. Think of the dollars I paid you for the story. Think of the documents I got you. Think of all those plastic coffins Jaime picked up.'

Alex didn't want to remember anything about them at all. He watched Oscar's sneering smile but Carlos came in quickly.

'I think of your generosity, Steve. I think of it all the time.'

Alex felt a spark of anxiety that steadily grew into a flame. Had Father Antonio been right? Could they really trust these men?

Maria took off her shoe and gingerly massaged her foot.

'We'll have something to eat,' said Carlos.

'What's the time?' Alex whispered to Paco, who pulled his watch slowly and lovingly out of his pocket.

'Just after ten. Let's say goodbye to Tijuana.' His voice was faint.

Alex glanced down at the lower end of the gully which was surrounded by rocky outcrops over which trails of mist were creeping. For a moment, he had the bizarre idea that the polluted atmosphere of the dump was following them like a cloud.

'Can we go down there?' Paco asked, seizing the initiative. 'We won't be seen.'

Oscar shrugged. 'You'd better not be,' he replied.

They leant against a huge boulder as Paco put his Ventolin spray to his mouth.

Scrubby, wiry grass grew starkly around them, the dusty foliage picked out in the pale moonlight. Shale moved beneath their feet, shifting and scraping together in little clouds of arid dust.

Paco was wheezing badly and Alex suddenly guessed why he wanted to get away. He could no longer control the asthma attack and didn't want the others to see.

But how could he help him? If Paco was beyond the relief of his inhaler, then what hope did he have? One fear had now quickly replaced another.

'Doesn't it work?' Alex asked, knowing how stupid he sounded.

Paco didn't reply, wheezing even worse than before and sitting down, shoulders heaving, knees drawn up to his chest.

A large set-piece firework from Tijuana lit the night sky. Unfortunately it resembled the Angel of Death, the Grim Reaper, complete with cloak and scythe. Car horns began to blast, a trumpet sounded and distant drums rolled. Night birds wheeled, disturbed by the tumult below, and a rat broke cover and scampered past them, heading for shelter in the baked earth of the Mesa.

Paco shook his spray but it seemed to be empty.

'Have mine.'

Paco grabbed it, put the nozzle in his mouth and began to squeeze.

Alex got to his feet. 'I'll fetch your mother.'

'No,' Paco hissed at him.

'Why not?'

'They'll leave me behind.'

Alex was certainly sympathetic to that particular feeling. Then he remembered how he had suffered a bad attack one night at home. Mum had called the doctor who said he was going to bring a nebuliser, a special machine that pumped Ventolin straight into the lungs. But he took over ten minutes to arrive, and during that dreadful time his mother had made Alex count each breath to try and relax him. Would that work with Paco? There wasn't much chance of ringing for a nebuliser on the Otay Mesa.

'Look. I've got this idea. Once I had a bad attack and I managed to control it by counting.' Alex was sure he sounded completely unconvincing and Paco looked up at him impatiently as he gabbled on. 'You count to three and take a long breath in. Then you count to three again and let your breath out. Got it?'

Paco shook his head.

'You've got to try.'

Paco was looking up at him blankly.

'You'll end up back in Tijuana. You'll never get to California.' He could have added, 'You'll never get better,' but Alex knew Paco realised that anyway. 'OK. We'll do it together.'

He grabbed Paco's wrist and felt his pulse which seemed to be racing at an incredible speed.

'You take a deep breath and hold it for – one – two – three.'

For a while Paco counted too quickly or too slowly and his breathing, if possible, got slightly worse until he was gasping like a stranded fish. He slapped away Alex's hold on his wrist, kicking out at him.

'Don't make it worse. Start counting. One, two, three – now breathe in and hold it. One, two, three. You can do it. You've *got* to do it.'

Paco's eyes were wider now, the fear flickering, his mouth open, sweat pouring down his face, a fist drumming against the rock. More fireworks soared over their heads, this time a cluster of dancing, mocking skeletons. It was as if Tijuana was laughing at Paco for trying to get away.

'Let's do it again. Trust me and do what I say.'

Slowly, miraculously, Paco's breathing began to ease.

'You feeling better?'

'I think so, but it's not a good night to cross. Those skeletons in the sky...'

'You can't be superstitious. It's only—' Alex broke off. 'What the hell are you two doing?'

Steve ran down the slope and Alex hurried into explanation.

'Paco had an asthma attack. A bad one. I was counting him down like Mum did for me once.'

'Counting?'

'Don't tell Carlos or Oscar. They could refuse to take us if they knew how bad the attack was.'

'Shouldn't I speak to your mother?'

'No. I must get to California.' There was terror in Paco's voice and Alex was sure that he would have another asthma attack if he got upset again.

Alex looked up at his father and said slowly, 'Leave him to me, Dad. I'll see he gets across.' As he spoke, he felt a sense of responsibility he had never felt before. The feeling was good.

'What have you been doing?' asked Oscar suspiciously, his smile widening.

'Watching the fireworks,' said Alex.

'Paco doesn't look so good.'

'I had too much beer.'

Alex watched Oscar whisper something to Carlos. The moonlight filled the gully, turning the ground a bleached white. Cristina was binding up Maria's foot and his father was unpacking some food from his rucksack. Everything *seems* all right, thought Alex, but now he felt cold with apprehension.

They ate some tacos and drank some of the bottled water, but there seemed to be no sign from their guides that they should move on.

Eventually Steve intervened. 'Isn't it time to...'

'Not yet,' said Carlos. 'We know the pattern of the flights.'

But we haven't even *heard* a helicopter, thought Alex, let alone seen one.

There was a long, uncomfortable silence.

'Trust us.' Oscar's smile broadened slightly. 'You have

paid us well and we have responsibilities. Like your son.'

'He's not making any difference,' snapped Steve.

'He is an additional member of the expedition. We have to be careful. Trust us,' he repeated.

'I don't see we have any choice,' stated Cristina. But Alex knew she was becoming increasingly uneasy. 'How much longer do we have to wait? And where are your famous helicopters? If this is the level of the American surveillance, there should be hundreds of our people jumping the fence.'

'It's not as easy as that,' said Carlos and then went into a stream of Spanish.

When he had finished, Maria laughed. 'I don't trust anyone,' she said. 'And particularly not you, Carlos.'

Steve took out his camera as if to defuse the mounting tension. As his father shot more film, Alex watched Carlos rummaging in his pocket, eventually dragging out a couple of skeleton carnival masks. He pulled his on and gave the other to Oscar. 'Now we can be photographed.' He laughed uproariously and the tension eased as they all gathered together, packed tightly into the frame with Carlos and Oscar flanking them, arms affectionately round each other's shoulders.

Looking down Alex saw a marigold petal.

'Now I take you,' said Oscar, his smile broader than ever.

Steve handed him the camera, explaining how the flash

worked, but Oscar nodded impatiently and asked him to join the by now giggling group. Alex wondered if he would keep the photograph to remind himself of the adventure he had shared with his father. What kind of memories would it bring back? Would he put it on his bedside table? Would Mum want a copy?

'Watch the birdie!' Oscar took several shots, then stepped back and stood in the shadows watching them. As he did so, Alex began to feel slightly bewildered. Was he going to take more photographs? From a different angle?

Then, slowly and with great deliberation, Oscar threw the camera to the ground.

There was a crunching sound and then a deafening silence.

SEVEN

Some small animal scuttled through the chaparral and a startled bird fluttered up from behind a spiky bush.

Steve gazed at his shattered camera, shaking his head, completely bewildered.

'You crazy?' demanded Cristina.

Carlos casually strolled over to join Oscar. They were still wearing their skeleton masks and there was a strange air of relaxed triumph about both of them, as if they had been building up to this macabre moment for a long time.

Now it had come.

'No,' said Maria. 'He's not crazy.' Her voice was full of bitter despair.

Oscar dug in his pocket as if he was going to show them a trick like the magician Alex had once watched with his mother.

He had never seen a gun in real life before. Alex gazed at the small, snub-nosed weapon which looked like a toy, incapable of doing damage. Would it shoot streamers? Was it a water-pistol? It *had* to be a joke.

He felt a leaden numbing in the pit of his stomach. Please, God, let Oscar be showing off, playing some silly game. Father Antonio mustn't be right.

Cristina began to yell at the coyotes in Spanish.

Oscar still said nothing, watching their reactions, pulling off his mask while Carlos did the same. The gully was completely still; there was no wind and the sound of the carnival at Tijuana was muted. Another small animal scrabbled and ran behind them.

Alex saw his father shrug hopelessly.

Carlos was gazing down at the ground, at the dirty blankets and the debris, anywhere but at the group that were still absurdly posed for their photograph.

'Carlos will check out the rucksacks,' said Oscar. 'Please don't do anything stupid.'

'I'll pay you more. Anything you want.' Steve's voice was only just under control.

The men ignored him. Carlos picked up Steve's rucksack first, emptying it out and putting the photographic equipment on one side.

Alex wondered what his father was going to do. He glanced at Cristina, but she and Maria were staring ahead without expression. Paco was wheezing.

Carlos gave a grunt of satisfaction as he found a wallet stuffed with dollar bills.

Cristina turned to Steve in contempt. 'You chose well. So-called coyotes who rob their own people.'

'They were recommended...' Steve started to try and bargain again. 'My magazine can make this really worth your while. You'll get far more...'

'I don't think so,' interrupted Carlos.

'You won't be safe in Tijuana,' Cristina yelled at him. 'My family will see to that.'

'We're not worried.' He chuckled. 'We're moving on.'

Alex knew that his father was deeply shocked but he didn't feel sorry for him. He had paid a fortune to a couple of crooks just because he wanted to be in charge like he always did.

Everyone had suspected Carlos and Oscar and they had been right. Dead right.

Thanks to his own stupidity, Steve was being robbed of a small fortune. There would be no shoot for *Atlas* magazine. Worse still, Paco would never see California.

Alex swung round as he heard a noise on the hard scrubby ground. Maria was running towards the two coyotes, her eyes blazing with fury, moving too fast for anyone to try and stop her. In seconds she had reached Oscar, ignoring the gun and raking his face with her fingernails.

He pushed her away, but she attacked him again while Alex stood by petrified.

Then Oscar hit Maria round the head with the butt.

She almost fell but just saved herself, staggering back to her mother. This was nothing like the level of violence he had seen on TV, but terrifying all the same.

'Give me the gun.' Now Steve began to move towards Oscar, who gazed at him in surprise, for once disconcerted.

Alex was appalled. Surely his father couldn't be playing the hero? Didn't he realise his game was over?

The shot was deafening in the silent canyon and birds high up in the rocky hillside made raucous cawing sounds as Steve stared down at the rising plume of dust on the ground.

Then, to Alex's disbelief, Steve started to move again. Didn't he know this was for real? The shot would ring out any minute and his father would lie dead in these bare brown hills. People would come and clear him away, throw his body on the dump where it would burn until all that was left were his carbonised legs, sticking up like fencing posts, pointing towards an overcast sky.

Steve had his hand out now, demanding the gun, and Alex suddenly wondered if by some miracle the risk would pay off. Was he really looking at a hero when he had been convinced for so long his father was a fake?

The shot seemed even louder this time and Alex watched Steve crumple up, clutching at his arm, making little moaning sounds. It was as if he was acting or still playing a game for them all to watch and applaud. Alex couldn't see any blood as his father fell to the dusty ground with a little gasp that sounded more like astonishment than pain.

Alex began to shake.

Paco grabbed at him, but he shook him off and rushed towards his father, while Oscar and Carlos watched, their expressions blank, as if the situation had moved out of their control and they were not sure what to do next.

Cristina took Maria in her arms and began to sob, but Alex hardly heard her as he knelt down beside his father who was lying on his side with his legs drawn up, making no sound at all. His shirt sleeve had a large hole in it and dark blood was pumping through.

'Don't move.' Alex only just managed to get the words out. 'You mustn't move.' The horror of it all was in the small things. A lizard scampered over Steve's ankle. Fireworks continued to resound from below as a rocket sent up coloured stars into the star torn sky. His father's wedding ring glinted in the pallid light of the moon. Then Steve's right hand clasped his arm protectively as the blood came through his fingers.

Cristina pushed Alex away, yelling at Oscar and Carlos, 'Give me a shirt – now!'

They stared at her blankly. Then Carlos rooted around in Steve's rucksack and threw one at her.

'That's not enough. I need more.'

He found another couple of shirts and she began to rip

them apart, eventually giving Alex a strip.

'You push that into the wound. Do you understand? You have to *push* it in. We need to stop the blood.'

'Let me help him,' pleaded Paco as Alex hesitated.

'No,' Cristina yelled at him. 'There's no time. Do what I tell you. Do it now.'

'I can't.' He hadn't even managed to pull his father's hand away from his arm, and in the end it was Cristina who dragged it off.

'You tear up the shirts. I'll stop the blood.'

Sobbing, tears streaming down his face, Alex watched Cristina press the material gently into the ragged hole in his father's arm. The wound seemed large and deep and there was no sign of the bullet. Steve gave a terrible cry. Not daring to look into his eyes, Alex tore up more of the shirt and Cristina rammed it in again.

His father screamed and went on screaming.

Alex turned to see Oscar examining one of the cameras he was about to steal, totally ignoring Steve's injury. Watch the birdie. The ridiculous phrase repeated itself over and over again in Alex's mind. Watch the birdie. Watch the blood.

He tore another shirt into longer, narrower strips and gave them to Cristina so she could keep the wadding in place. As she did so, Alex saw Oscar and Carlos stuff the money and photographic equipment back into one of the rucksacks.

Then Carlos picked up their loot and without looking back the two coyotes began to hurry away.

Alex stood up and ran after them. No one tried to stop him. His father had stopped screaming and was making a whimpering sound.

'You can't leave him.' Alex grabbed at Carlos's arm. 'He'll die. You've *got* to help us.'

Carlos tried to push him away, but Alex clung on as he was dragged down the rock-strewn trail.

'There is nothing we can do.' Carlos came to a halt, giving Oscar the rucksack with his free hand. 'He shouldn't have attacked us.'

'You shot him! You have to help us.'

'I can't help you. Only the Virgin Mary can do that.'

Then Carlos punched Alex in the stomach and he lost his grip, gasping for air, bent double as the two men began to run down the hillside.

After a few moments he slowly straightened up and staggered back to his father, kneeling down again beside him. Maybe I *should* pray, Alex thought. Maybe that's the only thing left to do.

EIGHT

'We'll have to go back,' Cristina was saying.

'No chance.' Amazingly, Steve seemed to be back in control again.

'You can't go on, Dad.' Alex was determined to sound calm, but he knew his voice was shaking. He looked down at his own hands and saw they were covered in his father's blood.

'We *are* going on. Aren't we, Alex?'

Suddenly his father was appealing to him, wanting his help as he had never wanted it before.

'If you can manage, Dad,' Alex said doubtfully, the words sticking in his mouth. He could see the sweat standing out on his father's forehead. A few minutes ago he had seemed to be in the most agonising pain; now he was trying to sit up. His determination was incredible.

'I told you to call me Steve,' he gasped.

'But I don't want to call you Steve,' Alex muttered. 'I want to call you Dad.'

'I would only call him a fool.' Cristina's voice was harsh, unforgiving and seemingly suddenly uncaring. 'That's all he ever was. This would never have happened if he hadn't let them talk him into paying up-front.'

'Aren't we going to California?' asked Paco miserably, as if he were a small child being deprived of a treat.

'Don't worry.' Steve tried to lever himself off the ground. 'We *are* going to California.'

Groaning and wincing with pain, he dragged himself to his feet and stood there, swaying slightly.

'Look.' Steve raised his arm with difficulty. 'No blood.'

Alex glanced at Cristina.

'We're not going anywhere,' she said flatly.

Paco began to pick up some T-shirts that were strewn about the ground, accidentally mixing them up with the filthy blankets.

'Put those back,' his mother yelled. 'They don't belong to us.' She paused, scowling at him, close to tears. 'I don't want to go on. At least we're safe in Tijuana.'

'*I* need to see a doctor.' Maria was yelling as loudly as her mother. What with the shots and now all this shouting, Alex reckoned the Border Patrol must be all too aware of their presence and heading towards them fast.

Steve was staggering slowly around the gully. His right hand had gone back to his arm and he kept arching his back. Alex didn't know what to do. His father was relying on him. He *had* to support him.

'How can you get us across in your condition? That's a really nasty wound and I'm sure the bullet's still in there somewhere.' Cristina spoke calmly now. Perhaps Steve would accept the logic of their situation.

'What about Paco's asthma?' asked Alex. 'Have you thought about him?'

'It's none of your business.' Cristina suddenly blazed at him.

'Don't speak to my son like that.' Steve said forcefully.

'Don't you care—'

'Paco needs treatment and he'll get it in Tijuana.'

'You haven't got the money.'

'I'll find it. I wouldn't have the money in America either, would I?'

'The air's better. There's no pollution.'

'He needs treatment. A specialist. Not just fresh air.'

'You *know* he'll die if he goes back,' said Alex bleakly. He no longer felt a child. He was one of the expedition, one of the adults, and they were behaving far more foolishly than any child.

Paco gazed down at the ground.

'He's not going to die.' Cristina was defensive.

'You mean, we're *not* going to California?' said Paco brokenly. 'We're near the border. We've got to go.' He was desperate. 'I had asthma bad when I was with Alex. He taught me how to count.'

'*Count?*' demanded Cristina. 'Count what?'

'I get asthma too,' said Alex. 'You count – my mother showed me. When you get a bad attack, you count your breathing. That stops you panicking.'

His mother gazed at Paco in concern. 'It was bad back there?'

'Yes.'

'Why didn't you tell me?'

'I was afraid Carlos and Oscar would leave me behind. Or not take any of us.'

'They were planning that anyway,' said Maria bitterly.

Cristina was watching Steve. 'He won't make it.'

But Alex could sense that she was weakening and raw fear surged through him. She was right. But he also knew his father's eyes were on him, demanding obedience.

'He'll manage,' Alex said. 'I'll make sure he does.'

'You're as big a fool as he is.' Cristina turned away, but Alex took the statement as a compliment. For once in his life Alex felt needed.

Picking up the remaining rucksacks and stuffing back what was left of their belongings the depleted expedition set out again, walking uphill, following a track that led them out of the protection of the gully and back on to the ridge.

On one side, Alex could see the lights of Tijuana, on the other the bejewelled palaces that were the multicoloured skyscrapers of San Diego, California. They were walking between two worlds and he knew he had no claim on either. Both were alien. Both hostile.

A lizard darted across a patch of loose shale in front of him and Alex felt a sharp stab of homesickness. He saw Winchelsea with its partly ruined church, sunlight playing on the grass and among the gravestones. The greenness of the memory made tears start in his eyes and he nearly slipped as yet another dry stone rolled treacherously into his path.

The Otay Mesa was sharply etched in the moonlight. Shadows seemed to move in the scrub, and Alex had the impression of being watched. The full moon was too bright, the sky studded with penetrating stars, the glittering canopy threatening in its clarity.

Then Alex saw Cristina drop another marigold petal.

Repeated images of his father walking steadily towards Oscar and then crumpling to the ground filled Alex's head. Whether he had been brave or simply foolish didn't matter. All Alex knew was that he loved him, that he was precious and he couldn't let him go.

But how could he help him? Had Cristina been right after all? Why had he been stupid enough to follow his father rather than her?

Paco wasn't going to die from his asthma, was he? At

least not right now. Who knew what was happening to the wound in Steve's arm? The bullet must be deeply embedded. Why hadn't they turned round and gone back to Tijuana? Steve. Father. Steve. Father. The names began to merge, to be one. There were no longer two people. The unknown, frightening Steve. The long-lost, hoped-for father. There was only one person now.

Gazing ahead, Alex had the feeling that they were walking over the top of the world, away from the stinking dump with its carbonised animals to the white sands of a Californian beach as if they were on the rim of a slowly turning wheel. Then he saw the fence silhouetted against the night sky, and knew the dreaming had to stop.

They had reached the border faster than he had imagined, a sharp ridge, made almost invisible by the folds of the brown hills. The fence, which looked well over ten feet tall, was one of the ugliest and most sinister sights Alex had ever seen. Rusty and stark, it stretched for miles and seemed to be built with battered sheeting.

'What's it made out of?' he whispered.

'They're landing mats,' muttered Steve. 'They're normally used by the US military for runways on temporary air bases − second-hand goods from the Pentagon.' He tried to laugh but all that came out was a painful coughing.

'They said some of it got washed away,' complained Maria.

'They were just a couple of crooks.'

'Pity you didn't realise that sooner.'

Exhausted, deeply concerned for his father, fearful of what was to happen next, Alex lost his temper. 'Why don't you just shut up and leave him alone?'

'What do *you* know of your father?' Maria sneered.

'Be quiet!' said Cristina sharply. 'This is the wrong time.'

'No it isn't.' Alex had worked himself up into a blind fury. 'I can't think why he bothered to have anything to do with you.'

'We're just trash on the dump, are we?' Before he could move, Maria raised her hand as if to hit him. Then she let it drop to her side.

But already Paco had pushed past his sister, his fists clenched. 'You call us scum?'

'No—'

'Dirt from the dump?'

'Calm down, Paco.' Cristina's voice rose. 'He didn't mean anything. We're going across the border. It's what you wanted.'

But Paco was already rushing at Alex, his fists swinging wildly.

'You see,' Cristina said to Steve who was swaying

slightly and still holding on to his arm. 'He doesn't obey me. Like *your* son, he won't do as he's told.'

Alex deflected some of Paco's blows as best he could, but he had underestimated how strong he was.

'I didn't call you anything,' he gasped. 'I want us to be friends.'

'But do you want to be my brother?' Paco stopped swinging at him for a moment and Alex remembered how he had punched at his father, maybe for much the same reason.

'Yes.'

He was surprised by what he had just said.

'You do?'

'I want to be your brother.'

They gazed at each other, not knowing what to do next. Then Paco slowly unbunched his fists and Alex could hear him beginning to wheeze.

'I'm sorry I can't knock these guys' heads together.' Steve put his good arm round Cristina and she rested her head on his shoulder.

'Is it true?' Alex asked. 'Are you two going to live together? If you are – you'll have to divorce Mum.' Tears came to his eyes as he said this, and his voice cracked.

Paco and Maria gazed at him anxiously – but Steve detached himself from Cristina and stared intently at the fence ahead of them.

Cristina drew Alex to her, stroking his hair and making

little murmuring sounds that were deeply comforting, almost as if she was his own mother and had always been so. He felt utterly confused, not able to separate one from the other. Then something snapped inside as he mentally forced them apart.

'Nothing is settled,' Cristina said, continuing to stroke his hair gently. 'We haven't even got across the border yet. I've grown fond of your father. Like most men he has many faults. But he wants to be needed. He wants *us* to need him, and we do.'

'I don't,' said Maria.

Cristina ignored her. 'She doesn't have my experience. Their father disappeared a long time ago and Maria still misses him. Paco needs Steve more than she does. I'm sorry, Alex – very sorry about your mother at home. I don't know how it'll be across the border. I'm a poor woman without papers.'

She's almost pleading, thought Alex. She needs me like she needs Dad. His tears had gone. In his mind he saw his mother standing on the hillside, watching them, shaking her head, the battered old shopping trolley at her side.

NINE

Steve's face was greyish-white in the moonlight and his hand was still pressed hard to his left arm. 'OK. Alex and Cristina are the only able-bodied members of this expedition.'

'I'm OK.' Paco was indignant.

'Shut up and do what I tell you.'

Surprisingly Paco didn't argue.

'I'm going to take a look at the fence.'

'Cristina and I can do that, Dad.' Alex was much more assertive now. 'You said we were the only—'

'You shut up too. I'm still in charge.'

He remembered waiting for his father in the café. Would he come back this time? Alex realised he was as unsure of him as ever, but this time for a different reason. Suppose the bullet was poisoning him and he just keeled over and died up there?

'I'll be back,' said Steve, looking at him steadily, and Alex knew he understood what he had been thinking.

'Be careful.'

Steve nodded and began to climb slowly up towards the fence, staggering a little as he went.

Cristina took out the remaining water bottles and Paco and Alex sipped slowly, holding each drop luxuriously in their mouths while she checked Maria's head.

'We'll be in America soon. In California,' Paco wheezed, but it was more of a question than a statement.

'Steve to the rescue.' Alex tried to sound confident.

Cristina left Maria and clasped her son's forehead. 'You have a fever?'

'No.'

'I've never heard you wheeze like this.'

'I'm OK.'

She stood looking up at the fence, the rusty sheeting dark in the moonlight. Alex wondered if she was praying. He leant against his rucksack, rigid with tension.

Paco seemed restless, checking in his pockets and riffling through the rucksacks. Eventually he slumped down beside Alex, whispering, 'My sprays are getting used up.'

'Doesn't your mother have any more?'

'No.'

'How much is left in the one you've got?'

'Not much. Do you have any?'

'I've got two but one's almost finished.'

'Don't tell my mother. If she knows, she'll go back.'

'You can have mine.'

'I know.' Paco grinned at him. But his chest was heaving again.

'What are you two talking about?' Maria's voice was suspicious.

'California,' said Paco.

'Don't let him trick you – like his father did.'

'My father didn't trick anyone,' snapped Alex, and then felt sorry, understanding her jealousy and aware of his own confused loyalties.

'California,' muttered Maria. 'It'll be as bad as the dump.'

'No, it won't,' wheezed Paco. 'I'll be able to breathe there, won't I?' He looked down at his watch. 'It's midnight,' he gasped. 'Luis will be waking up. He'll be going back to the house. He'll follow the marigold trail. Luis will be coming over the border with us. Won't he, Alex?'

There was no hesitation in his voice when Alex replied. 'He'll be coming, Paco.'

Cristina came over to sit by him. 'What do you think your father wants to do with his life?'

Alex was surprised that Cristina was consulting him. He certainly couldn't answer her, although he also felt flattered to be asked. An adult had never needed his opinion before and he was afraid he was going to disappoint her.

'I don't know.' Alex sought refuge in ignorance.

But she wasn't really listening and he realised she wanted to talk, to get her own thoughts in some kind of order.

'At first I thought Steve just wanted to use us. He met my brother Manuel in the cathedral and asked him if he knew of a family who wanted to get across the border. He said his magazine would pay, providing there was a photographic record – like a good story for the readers. Manuel thought of us, but he was careful. He didn't want to give too much away. Then there was Paco.'

Cristina paused and then said bitterly, 'But Steve didn't tell me he was married. He didn't tell me he had a son.'

A hollow feeling grew inside Alex. *What do you think your father wants to do with his life?* The question began to beat in his head. Suddenly Steve appeared again. Steve the stranger. His father seemed a long way away.

'I'm an educated woman.' Cristina was defensive. 'I went to a convent school. My father owned a fishing trawler but he's dead now and so is my mother. Manuel didn't want to fish so he sold the boat. What a fool he was. I could have helped run the business just as my mother helped my father. We got poor. It's like a wasting disease. You go down and down until you reach the dump. In a way Steve was the angel of mercy, come at last. Or so it seemed at first.'

Alex gazed around him, at Paco who had fallen asleep, at Maria gazing sullenly up at the wire, at Cristina's bitterness. Were they just his father's puppets? Then he saw Steve's shadow stumbling down the hillside and felt a bitter resentment – not against his father but Cristina. How could she talk about him like that when he was still fighting for her, despite what Carlos had done to him?

'He's coming,' Cristina said almost eagerly. Then she looked away, ashamed that she needed him and even more ashamed that Alex knew.

'Someone's started to dig under the fence, but there's a long way to go. We're going to have to move fast.' Steve was out of breath and wincing with pain. He glanced down at Paco who had woken suddenly.

'When are we going to be in California?' Paco's voice was childish and blurred with sleep. Maria put her arm round him and began to rock her brother like a baby.

A chilly night breeze was blowing but they were all sweating as Steve's torch played on a shallow excavation under the fence where it looked as if someone had started digging but given up.

'If we get some flat stones, I think we could make more of an impression.' He winced and Alex saw the stain that was spreading through the improvised bandages. Should he tell Cristina? Had she noticed his father's arm was bleeding again?

'That's the way to California?' said Paco flatly.

Cristina kissed him, listening fearfully to his rattling wheeze. 'California here we come!' she announced.

Alex glanced round anxiously. The moon cast a pale glow over the border, turning rock and shale soft and shifting, rather as if they were waves on a milky ocean.

'Dad, you've got to drive later,' Alex reminded his father.

'You mustn't make yourself –' He was going to say 'worse', but he hurriedly substituted the word 'tired'.

His father nodded, as if for once aware of his limitations. He gave a low groan and then dragged his hand away from its now all too familiar place around his arm.

Then Cristina took over. 'Alex and I will dig and Maria will take the earth.'

'What about me?' wheezed Paco unhappily. 'I've got nothing to do.'

'You have to look after Steve.'

Under her command the expedition was united for the first time.

Alex began to search for flat stones, and after some difficulty came up with a couple that everyone looked at doubtfully. They only had a few hours. With such inadequate tools, they could be digging for weeks.

A wave of hopelessness swept over him, and when he looked up at his father he saw that his eyes were those of a little boy who realised the game had got too big for him. His face was gaunt and there was so much sweat on his forehead that it couldn't possibly have come from the exertion.

Predictably, the flat stones made little impression on the hard rocky ground. Above them, the iron sheeting rose bleakly, jaggedly silhouetted against the night sky.

'We need something sharper.' Cristina got up stiffly, looking around her.

Alex spotted something metallic in the gully below them. He clambered down and, scrabbling around, eventually held up a rusty metal cup.

'Well done there,' said Steve, sounding like a hearty scout master, but Alex could see that his face was screwed up in pain and his grey pallor had increased. The stain on the bandages was darker and deeper.

'You're bleeding, Steve,' said Cristina softly. 'I need to dress that wound again and make you a sling to rest your arm in.'

'We haven't got time.'

'Don't lose any more blood, Dad. You won't make it...'

His father sat down suddenly, his lips compressed, and Cristina began to pull off the sticky mass of bandage. As she did so, he began to whimper. The sound was dreadful to hear.

'Give me your other hand, Steve,' said Maria awkwardly. 'You squeeze mine.'

'I'll dig,' said Alex, not wanting to watch.

Neither did Paco. 'We'll take turns,' he said.

'No – you keep away.' Alex spoke harshly, wanting to hurt and succeeding.

Alex returned to the fence and began to dig in a swirl of dust, trying to ward off the sound of his father's pain, but hearing him cry out and over again.

'Please.' Cristina was pleading. 'You must be quiet.'

'I'm sorry.'

'I know.'

'I won't—' And the terrible scream came again, high and shrill, like an animal in a trap.

'I think the wound's got infected,' said Cristina quietly. 'Don't forget the bullet's still in there.'

'Infected?' Steve's voice was harsh. 'In such a short time?' But he sounded defeated.

Alex began to dig even harder, scraping at the flinty earth with his metal cup and throwing the debris behind him, his breathing loud and harsh. But at least he didn't have asthma, despite the dust. He *had* to keep digging. He *had* to shut out his father's agony.

He went on digging for over five minutes until Paco roughly grabbed his shoulder.

Alex shook him off. 'I've got to keep going.'

'It's one o'clock. How long is this going to take? Until dawn? Let me take my turn.'

'OK.' Alex gave in.

The two boys worked on a five-minute rota, shovelling as hard as they could.

'The wound's deeper than I thought,' Alex heard Cristina whisper to his father.

'Shut up and plug it,' he told her.

Steve sat up against a rock, his eyes closed and his chest heaving while Maria and Cristina began to take their turns with the digging. But the job was still slow because there was only room for one person to scrape away with the metal cup in the gap under the fence.

They worked away for the next two hours, until Alex could taste the flinty earth in his mouth, feel it filling his ears and nose.

The fireworks still trailed above them. Processions of skeletons glittered in the night sky and then a huge skull glared malevolently down at them.

Eventually, straightening up, Alex realised they had made a much deeper impression than he had imagined.

'We're almost there!'

His father's eyes were closed, and he nodded but didn't speak.

'Are you still bleeding?' Alex had reached a new pinnacle of fearful despair. This was all crazy. How could any of them expect Steve to keep going with an injury like that?

'I'm fine,' he replied, sounding ludicrous.

'You haven't answered...'

'Cristina's done a good job.' As if to stop the questions, his father forced himself to his feet, gasping with pain. 'How's Paco?'

'Not so good.'

The other boy was sitting on the ground, his shoulders heaving, gazing down at his new watch as if it was a good-luck charm.

'That counting – did you say your mother taught you?'

'Yes.'

Steve frowned. 'I don't seem to have had much of a hand in your life, do I?'

'No.'

He moved slowly away, his head bowed.

TEN

The relentless digging continued. Alex's nails were broken and his fingers torn and bleeding. But still he worked on, his arms stiff and aching, wrists sore, fingers numb.

The scraping seemed to be inside him now, as if his mind was full of it, and his mouth was so dry that it was almost impossible to swallow. How long had they been digging? All he could think about now was water – ice-cold – in a bottle that had a shadowy chill on the outside.

He fantasised that he was holding the liquid up to the light, seeing the bubbles. Soon he would unscrew the cap and put the bottle to his lips, slaking his thirst.

Alex fought against the tantalising images and dug and scraped even harder, until he was stopped by a sharp and terrible pain that made him whimper aloud, as if every nerve in his body had been jangled.

Peering down at his hand, he saw that a large splinter

from a buried piece of wood had got under one of his nails. He yanked it out and then, like an automaton, returned to his task.

'Stop!' Steve had a hand on his shoulder.

Alex came to a shuddering halt, every muscle burning.

'We're through. You've made it!'

Somehow Alex crawled out of the hole and grabbed his water bottle, taking a long draught and then another.

'Don't drink it all. Have some of mine.'

'I can't do that.'

'You can. You will.'

Alex drank deeply, conscience dwarfed by his need. Eventually he stopped, guiltily looking at the heavily reduced level in his father's water bottle.

'You've done it, Alex. We've all done it.' Cristina's cheeks were flooded with tears and she kissed his sweating forehead over and over again. Then she took out the box and tossed a marigold petal under the fence.

'You OK?' Alex asked Paco.

'Sure I'm OK. I'm going to California, aren't I?'

Alex could see that he was breathing heavily. Could he really have a fever? Was that making his asthma so much worse? Perhaps it wasn't asthma at all. If he *did* have an infection then he'd need antibiotics and where could they get those from? And what about his father? Suppose Cristina was right and he had an infection too?

'I've been counting the seconds. On the watch. On *my* watch,' said Paco.

'We're going under the fence. We've got to hurry.'

'I'm ready.'

Cristina was by his side now. 'Come on. You can be the first to reach America.'

Paco was in a bad way now, but he made it. Alex went next and then Maria and Cristina. But the worst job was to pull Steve through without opening up his wound again.

'Turn on your right side,' said Cristina. Her voice was gentle now.

Steve lay down and Cristina and Alex took hold of his right arm, leaving the damaged one still in its improvised sling.

'Push with your legs, Dad.'

He tried, but the whimpering that Alex couldn't bear to hear began again.

'I can't do it.'

'You must,' said Cristina.

'You've got to,' added Alex fiercely. 'It won't take long if you just shove. Come on!'

Steve tried again and gave a high-pitched squealing sound that was even worse than the whimpering. It must hurt like hell, thought Alex. Were they killing him – trying to get his father over the border like this?

'Shove!' he yelled despite all his qualms. 'Shove, Steve.'

'I'm trying to.'

But he wasn't. It was just like Paco and his refusal to count. What was the matter with them? Why didn't they do what he said?

'You're not. Come on, push and we'll pull.'

'He is right, Steve. You have to try. However much it hurts you have to try very hard,' hissed Cristina.

Between them, they somehow hauled him under the fence. Once he was through, Steve lay in the dust, the blood welling up through the bandages yet again, staining the sling a dull crimson.

'We'll have to stop that bleeding,' Cristina said to Alex as if they were close friends who had been through hell together. 'The problem is that we're running out of stuff we can use as bandages.'

Then they heard Maria's voice. 'Take my blouse. I've got a sweater.' From being soundly abused, Steve was now being anxiously looked after.

'This is going to hurt again,' said Cristina as she knelt beside him.

'Take my hand, Dad,' said Alex, getting there just before Maria. 'Squeeze hard.'

Twenty minutes later, Steve rose painfully to his feet and they all stood for a moment staring down into the darkness that was slashed by a distant freeway running towards San Diego.

'We're here,' wheezed Paco. 'We got to California.'

There was a short silence.

Cristina began to cry and Steve put his good arm awkwardly round her. 'Happy?' he asked.

'I don't know,' she sobbed and he held her close. 'Do you think Luis will find the way? Will he follow the petals?'

Alex bit his lip and looked away.

They walked on for a while in silence, hardly able to believe that they had actually succeeded in making the crossing.

Paco was the most joyful of them all, and soon he could be heard singing snatches of *California here I come!*

Maria had relaxed, and Cristina seemed to have regained her respect for Steve.

But Alex had also noticed that Steve's right hand was pressed even more tightly against his left arm, trying to ease the pain. His eyes seemed glazed, there were flecks of saliva at the corners of his mouth. Was the wound going septic? How long could he keep going? Yet again, Alex seriously considered the awful possibility of his father not making it. He tried to push the thought away but it kept coming back.

Finally, as Cristina began to stride out ahead Alex managed to whisper, 'Are you still bleeding?'

'Not much.'

'How far is the truck?'

'About a mile.'

'Do you want to lean on me?'

'I'm fine.' But his father was biting his underlip and Alex knew every step was agonising.

They were passing across the top of a small ravine full of rubbish and smelling of urine. Black plastic bags and a couple of old gas burners, blankets, cans and broken wood were piled up on its floor. Some of the stuff had been burnt and a cindery smell competed with the urine.

Once again, the image of a battleground entered Alex's mind as a glimpse of grey dawn began to lighten the night sky. 'I don't want anything to happen to you,' Alex blurted out.

'It won't.'

'You're gritting your teeth.'

'So would you be if someone shot you. But thanks to Cristina I haven't lost too much blood and I'm going to be OK.'

'You need a doctor.'

'Believe me, Alex, the worst is over.'

But was it? In the cold dawn light, Alex was assailed by doubts and unfamiliar fears.

ELEVEN

'What's that noise?' Alex whispered. They were on the undulating slope of the rocky landscape now, looking down into a wasteland of scrub that disappeared into darkness.

'I didn't hear anything.'

Cristina came up with Paco and Maria. 'What's the problem?'

'There *isn't* one,' snapped Steve. 'Alex thought he could hear something. But it's only his imagination.'

'Is it?' Cristina wasn't convinced. 'What *can* you hear? Is it that buzzing sound?'

'More like droning,' muttered Alex.

'Droning or buzzing. What the hell does it matter?' Steve was impatient. 'What are we waiting for? Killer bees?'

'There are lights up on the Mesa,' said Paco. 'Like little stars.' He pointed across the hills. 'It's like they're moving towards us.'

Steve cleared his throat. 'Sorry, Alex.'

'What is it, Dad?' he demanded fearfully.

'To hell with the stars,' his father yelled. 'Those are headlights and they're coming this way.'

The powerful beams blazed through the night as engines roared and dust flew. The little expedition cowered, shocked by the sudden invasion.

Were these Border Patrol vehicles, wondered Alex. Did they operate in convoy like this and in such a dramatic way? He noticed a couple of scattered marigold petals gleaming pale yellow and then soon lost to sight.

'Get down,' yelled Steve, pushing him to the ground.

The others followed, lying flat, knowing they were exposed and that there was no shelter. We're finished, Alex thought. After all we've been through we're going to be caught and taken back. Paco's asthma will get worse. He'll die and be buried near the dump, his corpse washed out with the floods.

The lights came nearer, following the line of the fence, and Alex could see half a dozen jeeps, a high-beam spotlight mounted on the cab of each vehicle. Inside were men in stocking masks and combat jackets, some carrying flashlights and radios. Did the Border Patrol dress in this paramilitary way?

The jeeps roared on, either ignoring or not seeing them, driving three abreast, their spotlights picking out each boulder, each scrubby bush.

'Who are they?' Alex demanded. 'The Border Patrol?'

'No way,' replied Steve. 'They're a neo-Nazi group who call themselves the Aryans. They've set themselves up as vigilantes. Maybe they're after another expedition who crossed over, but we can't hang around to find out. We must get to the truck fast.'

Then one of the jeeps separated from the small convoy and began to roar towards them.

'Dig in!' yelled Steve.

Dig into what, wondered Alex. His scrabbling fingers made no impression on the hard ground. Another of his nails broke and the sharp pain seemed to fill his entire body. He could hear Paco wheezing like a steam engine, so loudly that Alex had the ridiculous notion that he was drawing the jeep towards them. He could smell the acrid dust and diesel oil. Were they going to be run down?

Then, with a screaming of tyres, the jeep changed direction to rejoin the convoy. They hadn't been seen after all. Or, if they had, some game was being played.

Steve was already dragging himself to his feet. 'Let's go!' he yelled.

The jeeps were still in sight, their tail-lights gleaming red in the half-light that contained the first streaks of a pink dawn.

Alex slowed down, waiting for Paco, and as he did so there was a flash. The flames leapt along the line of the wire and he realised that the tinder-dry scrub had been set alight. With a fierce crackling, the fire spread and the jeeps began to back off at high speed.

'What are you doing?' yelled Steve, clutching at his arm. 'We've got to get away from here.'

'Paco can't run.'

'He must!'

Alex dragged at Paco's hand, but it was hot and damp and limp. He felt a numbing sense of hopelessness.

Steve swore while Cristina yelled, 'You've got to help him. You can't leave him.'

'I'm not going to.'

'I'll carry him,' shouted Maria, bending down, trying to scoop up her brother and staggering for a few seconds under his weight.

'No,' said Steve, pushing her away roughly and then wincing with pain. 'I'll take him.'

'Don't be an idiot, Dad,' yelled Alex. 'Of course you can't.' He turned to Paco and grabbed his hand again. 'Get up on my back. Now!'

Alex tried to run, his muscles screaming as Paco got heavier every stumbling step he took.

The fire had really taken hold now and the flames were running downhill, long red snakes that lashed and curled, until the debris as well as the scrub caught light, sending up clouds of choking black smoke. They could already smell it, toxic and suffocating, and however hard Alex ran, the fire pursued him faster, its heat searing.

Cristina tore at his shirt. 'Let me have Paco.'

Alex shook his head and then saw a sandy track, branching off to the left.

'That's where the truck is.' He came to a shuddering halt, his arms shaking. Behind them, the flames reared up and the crackling became more intense.

'For God's sake, give him to me.' Cristina held out her hands and Paco slipped down from Alex's back.

Relieved of his burden, hardly able to breathe, Alex waited for his father who was staggering along in the grey half-light, his face covered in sweat, lips moving, a hand inevitably clasped to his left arm. Just how long was he going to be able to keep going like this? It was a miracle he had got so far. Would he make the truck? More importantly, would he be able to drive?

The smoke was beginning to drift over them, dense and suffocating, strands lodging in their throats, the taste acrid, making them cough, hacking away until it hurt.

The track wound steeply downhill and the streaks of light were brightening the landscape, but it was still difficult to see what was beneath their feet.

Several times Alex almost fell. Then Cristina went down, pitching forward, dropping Paco. Unable to stop, Maria went with her, and they rolled over in a heap.

In the dim light Alex saw Paco lying on his back, his eyes wide open. Cristina took his wrist and shook her head. 'There's no pulse,' she said unbelievingly.

Paco's pale face showed not the slightest sign of life.

So he *is* dead, thought Alex. Dead at last. Like Luis.

'Of course there's a pulse.' Steve pushed Cristina aside and grabbed at Paco's wrist. 'I know what to do.' He sounded full of his usual determined authority.

Maria sobbed hysterically while Cristina continued to stare down incredulously at her son's open eyes.

Alex watched his father bend painfully over Paco, holding open his jaws with his right hand and blowing into his mouth.

'You killed him,' shouted Maria. 'It was your fault, Steve. Just because you wanted to make money out of us.' Her voice rose until she was screaming at him. 'You've killed Paco. Murdered him—'

Cristina grabbed Maria and shook her. 'You must be quiet. You *have* to be quiet.'

Alex also knew it was hopeless, that Paco was dead. Was Maria right? Was it all his father's fault? He was so exhausted he could hardly remember what had happened – or what they had been trying to achieve.

'I can't get him back,' yelled Steve, gazing up at Alex, terrified and unable to cope any longer. 'It's no good. I can't make him breathe—'

'You've got to!' Cristina's voice was hard and flat. 'You *said* you could.'

'Let me try,' Alex intervened. 'I know how to do it.'

Steve moved aside as Alex knelt down beside Paco and

forced open his mouth, pressing his lips tightly to his and breathing hard down his throat. When he had done this he began to pummel at his chest. Then Alex started the sequence all over again.

The spark of life was like the fluttering of a moth in distant darkness. A tiny shuddering, a minute exhalation of air. But then it came again and again, with gathering strength. His father must have done something wrong, thought Alex. Or had he just been lucky?

He was about to breathe down Paco's throat again when, to his amazement, he saw that there seemed to be no need. He had begun to breathe again with a gasping jolt and then the wheeze returned, almost like an old friend.

'You've got him back,' whispered Steve. 'You've got him back.' His eyes were dull with pain and confusion, but in that moment Alex knew for certain how much he loved and needed his father. Now, at last, their dependence was mutual. Elation filled him and he gazed down at Paco, unable to believe that he was breathing again – that he, Alex Carson, had *made* him breathe again.

'Hail, Mary,' Cristina was whispering. 'Hail, Mary, full of grace.'

Steve tried to re-establish his authority by urging them on. 'It's not far to the truck. We *must* get going.'

The smoke seemed to be hanging over the hillside rather than following them down the canyon, but Alex could hear the steady roar of the flames.

They got up stiffly and Cristina and Maria carried Paco between them. They'd kill to protect him, thought Alex. But then Paco would do the same for them if he could.

'At least you're not a bullshitter,' said Maria as she passed Alex. 'Unlike your father.'

'You should be grateful. He's risked everything for you lot. He got shot trying to protect you.'

'Steve took the risks for himself,' she sneered. 'Like he does everything.'

TWELVE

Alex recognised the place where they had hidden the truck and he ran towards the galvanised iron shack, pulling away the brittle scrub. Behind him the blazing Mesa was still cloaked in smoke and flame.

Once the truck was uncovered Alex helped Steve drag an old tarpaulin out of the back. His father tried to assert himself again, but now his voice was thin and weak. 'I want to make it look as if we're just fruit pickers driving to work – like we've done every day for the last few months. That way we won't be stopped.'

Paco was sitting on the ground, looking around him, seeing California properly for the first time, seemingly unaware of what had happened.

'My brother needs help,' said Maria. 'Medical help. Like now.'

Alex felt another flash of temper. They'd made it, hadn't they? Was it really his father's fault that he had been conned by Carlos and Oscar? Was it Steve's fault that he hadn't got the right technique for resuscitation? He'd tried, hadn't he? Why did these women have to make him look such a fool?

'I hope there'll be a doctor at the farm. There's nothing we can do until then.' Steve sounded uncertain.

'Suppose we *do* get stopped?' asked Cristina.

'You'll be back in Tijuana in a few hours.'

'Maybe that'll be a good thing,' observed Maria sourly.

'You're here, aren't you? You crossed the border. What more do you want?' Alex yelled, unable to control himself any longer.

Do you want my father, he thought, or will you kick him out of your lives now you've used him up? But Alex realised there was no point in Steve coming home defeated. He would only go away again.

'How long will the journey take?' asked Cristina.

'Just over an hour. I suggest you three get under the tarpaulin and Alex can come with me in the cab. We'll be less noticeable that way.' Steve looked at his watch. 'I'm going to wait for a few minutes and hope those jeeps get clear. Then we'll go.' He dragged himself on to the step of the truck and sat there, hunched up, the sweat running down his pallid face.

Alex went over to Paco.

'Are we *really* in California?' He seemed confused, his breathing ragged. 'My chest hurts,' he added, but Alex didn't want to tell him the reason why.

'We're going to the farm. It's going to be all right.'

'What happened to me?'

'You passed out,' he began but Cristina intervened.

'You must tell him the truth,' she insisted. 'You were unconscious and Alex gave you the kiss of life. It was a miracle. You came back to us.' Her voice broke. 'We lost Luis. We thought we'd lost you. You've been born again.'

Paco's eyelids fluttered and he didn't seem to hear. He's so weak, thought Alex. Just like Steve. Suppose Paco stopped breathing again before they reached the farm? It was a miracle he had been lucky enough to bring him back the first time. Alex was sure his luck wouldn't last if he had to do it again.

'You were scattering petals,' Alex said. 'For Luis?'

'You know about him?'

'Paco told me. Do you mind?'

Cristina pulled the box out of her jacket pocket. 'We do this for our festival – the Day of the Dead. The souls follow the marigold path back home. I thought Luis might follow us – to our new home.'

There was an awkward silence.

'I could only bring a few petals for him. I hope he'll find his way.' She glanced at Alex curiously. 'Do you believe?'

'I don't know. I'd like to...'

'You brought Paco back from the dead,' she insisted.

'I was lucky.'

'It's not luck. It's God. Working inside you.'

Alex found himself wishing she was right.

Paco began to mutter something in Spanish and Alex knelt down beside him. '*Que bonito es el mundo; ¡lastima yo tenga que morir!* I dreamt I was dead.'

You were, thought Alex. 'What do those words mean?'

'How beautiful the world is; it's a pity I must die.'

'You're not dying. No one's dying.' But he knew he was floundering. His father might die. Paco might die. After all, it *was* the Day of the Dead.

'I dreamt I was a soul following the marigold path, flying into my mother's house, looking for the *ofrenda* – the offering she and Maria had made on the table. Bread and water and milk and fruit and the tortillas with red chilli sauce and the drink of maize meal.'

'You're making me hungry.' Alex tried to joke and failed.

'What happens when you die?'

He said nothing, wondering if Paco was delirious. His breathing was still bad and he seemed to gasp for each breath. Shouldn't they both be counting? But he was so tired. Too tired to count any more. His father. Paco. They seemed beyond help.

'The *mole* is simmering, the bread is baked, the Day of the Dead is here. I want to tell you, Alex.'

'Tell me what?'

'I want to tell you. In your language. Not mine.'

'Why?'

'I want you to understand what I dreamt about. How I followed the marigold path.'

'OK,' Alex said at last. 'I breathed into your lungs. Then you weren't dead any longer.'

Paco reached out and took Alex's wrist. He was surprised by the strength of his grip.

'We should go,' said Steve, standing by the truck, looking back at the burning hillside, the smoke drifting up into the dawn sky.

'What about those vigilantes?'

'Over the other side of the Mesa, I hope.'

'Why do they do it?' asked Alex.

'Out of fear.'

'What's illegal immigration to them?'

'What were the Jews to the Nazis?'

'Shouldn't the Border Patrol be up there? *Doing* something?'

'Maybe they are. Or maybe they backed off. Either way, we have to get going.' Steve turned abruptly to Cristina. 'Get them under the tarpaulin.' His voice held a shaky return to his old authority and Alex wanted to give him as much support as he could. Didn't Cristina care about the bullet in his father's arm – the bullet he had got trying to protect her family?

THIRTEEN

Trying to move his left arm as little as possible, Steve backed the truck out and turned it round slowly in the narrow space and then bumped down the little track, the headlights picking out abandoned cars without wheels and a burnt-out camper van. Soon they were travelling down a narrow ravine with a steep drop on one side and shale and boulders on the other.

The vegetation was sparse and sentinel cacti loomed out of the rock, each looking like a monster gravestone, oppressive and threatening.

The daylight spread slowly over the shadowy landscape as the truck reached an intersection.

Alex thought he saw a dark shape crouching among the cacti. Then he dismissed it as yet another abandoned vehicle, and it was only when he glanced back through the wing mirror that he saw with sudden dread the jeep begin to follow them.

'Dad—'

'I've seen it.' His father put his foot down hard on the accelerator. 'For God's sake tell them to keep under that tarpaulin. I can see Maria poking her head out.'

Alex leant out of the window and yelled at her, noticing the jeep was gaining fast, coming up behind them, bonnet practically touching the rear fender of the pick-up. Then they were rammed. Steve fought for control, somehow using both hands, whimpering with pain, sweeping away from the edge of the ravine and skidding on loose shale, battling with the wheel until they were back in the middle of the track.

Then the jeep hit them again, but this time Steve was ready, changing down the gears, managing not to skid.

'He's coming alongside,' yelled Alex.

'Get down!'

He crouched in his seat and then hit his head painfully on the dashboard as his father braked hard.

Alex inched himself up to just above the level of the window and risked taking a look.

The young man's head was only a metre away from his own. He couldn't have been more than seventeen, clean-cut and tanned, his expression neutral, just as if he was passing the time of day rather than trying to force them into a ravine.

'Get down, for Christ's sake!'

As Alex ducked, the jeep hit the pick-up a glancing blow and then another. Now both vehicles were racing side by side along the narrow track, dust flying up into the grey dawn, Steve still managing to keep control, despite still using his injured arm.

'How far to the freeway?'

'Soon.' His father groaned with pain. Then the impact came again and Alex braced himself as one wheel of the pick-up left the dirt track. Somehow Steve got it back on the hard surface again.

Alex felt compelled to take another look at their attacker and found himself held by the frank, open gaze of the young man. Then their tormentor gave a thumbs-up sign as he veered towards them.

This time the impact was much greater. Steel ground steel and there was the screaming of metal as Steve still held grimly to the shaking wheel.

The bend came up fast. Too fast. Steve lost control as the pick-up skidded towards the ravine and Alex was sure they were going over. Instead the vehicle came to a jarring halt.

With an agonised gasp his father tried to back up, but the truck seemed to be stuck fast, the engine revving uselessly.

The young man got out and casually began to walk towards them.

He wrenched open the offside door of the truck and stood watching them, frowning slightly as if puzzled, a gun in his hand. It was much smaller than the weapon

Oscar had used but Alex knew that its size would make no difference. It would be just as lethal.

Steve was bent over the steering wheel now, not moving. Was he unconscious? Had the wound opened up again?

'Where are you folks going in such a hurry?'

'Leave us alone,' stammered Alex. 'We haven't done anything to you.' He sounded as if he were in a school playground, cringing from a bully.

The young man grinned. 'Am I the skeleton at the feast?' he asked. 'Am I interrupting a little All Souls' Day party?'

He must think Steve is dead drunk, thought Alex. Not just nearly dead. 'You've hurt him.'

'Looks like a gunshot wound he's got there,' said the young man in some surprise.

Alex looked down and saw the fresh red blood seeping down the filthy bandage on Steve's arm. Now he felt utter defeat. The expedition was over.

'Get out!'

'My father can't move. You've got to help him.' Alex's voice shook.

'Get out!'

Fleetingly, he wondered how much the bullets would hurt.

Then to Alex's utter bewilderment the young man began to topple backwards, dropping his gun as he fell to the track with Maria's strong hands around his throat.

They rolled about in the dirt as she clutched at his short brown hair, banging his head on the ground.

Alex jumped down from the truck and ran towards them, snatching up the gun and hurling it down into the ravine. Then he grabbed Maria round the waist and pulled her struggling and cursing off her victim, who lay groaning as Cristina stood over him.

Alex went to the jeep, took out the ignition keys and threw them into some bushes, feeling a wild, heady elation. He was powerful again.

The young man staggered to his feet, choking and wiping at the blood in his hair. Then he walked over and sat down heavily in his jeep.

'You've got to help me with your father,' Cristina was saying. 'He's real bad now. Can you hear me? You've got to help me.' Her voice shook and seemed very distant. Alex realised that she was talking to him.

Steve seemed to be barely conscious as Cristina, Maria and Alex tried to pull him as gently as they could out of the cab and into the back of the pick-up where they laid him under the tarpaulin, his head resting on Cristina's rolled-up sweater.

The process took a long time and they were all afraid of more jeeps arriving.

'We can't just leave that guy,' Alex said once Steve was settled. 'He needs help.'

'So does your father,' Cristina yelled at him. 'This wound's much worse – it's been torn open even more. I've got to stop the bleeding.'

Nevertheless, Alex ran across the track to the jeep while Cristina shouted at him to come back.

'Are you going to be OK?'

There was matted blood in the young man's hair. His eyes were wide and Alex could see the shock in them.

'I was making a citizen's arrest,' he muttered and Alex wondered how badly concussed he was.

'She didn't know that.'

'Alex,' yelled Cristina. 'If you don't come now, I'm driving away without you.'

'They're Mexican scum. They get into our country illegally. They're wrecking the economy, setting up organised crime—'

'Why don't you shut up!' Alex yelled at him.

'Go to hell,' replied the young man viciously.

Between them, Cristina, Maria and Alex managed to pull the truck off the large rock that had saved them from plunging into the ravine. Although the vehicle was damaged, Cristina was able to drive down to the freeway. Wouldn't they be arrested right away, Alex wondered – with the truck in the state it was and driven by an illegal immigrant? She took the inside lane, the battered coachwork rattling and something grinding away underneath.

'Are you sure you can drive this?' Alex asked uneasily, expecting a patrol car to pull them over at any minute.

But Cristina ignored him, gripping the wheel tightly. 'My sister sent me directions for the farm and I've memorised them.' She paused, reached into her jacket and tried to throw a few more marigold petals on to the freeway. But in doing so she swerved violently.

'Let me do that,' Alex suggested. The marigold path for Luis no longer seemed absurd. It was a necessity.

'Are you crazy? You sound just like your father. Always trying to do things you can't. Of course you can't drive.'

'I'm talking about scattering the marigolds. You nearly came off the road just then.'

Cristina handed over the box gratefully.

As he threw a couple of petals on to the freeway, Alex wondered if Steve needed a pathway home, just like Luis. But the tragedy was, however many marigold petals Alex threw, his father's spirit would have a problem knowing where home was. Then he pulled himself together. Steve was going to live. He *had* to live.

Cristina seemed to detect what Alex was feeling and put a hand on his arm, making the truck swerve again, but this time at least not so violently. Nevertheless, he was relieved when she gripped the wheel again.

'He'll get through,' she said.

'How do you know?'

'I've seen bad injuries on the dump. People live if they

have the will, and your father has plenty of that.'

Alex was silent for a long time. Then he asked, 'Do you love him?'

Cristina shrugged.

His eyes kept closing, however hard he forced them open. He tried to think but his brain seemed to be on hold, a great blank space that was gradually filled by images of the dump as he finally slept, his head on Cristina's shoulder, dreaming that the carbonised animals were prancing to the raucous tunes of the Day of the Dead.

He heard Paco's words again. How beautiful the world is. It's a pity I must die.

Gradually, another level of deep, merciful, dreamless sleep seized him.

FOURTEEN

'We're here,' Cristina said gently.

The battered truck was parked in a grove of small oak trees. It was still early morning with a slight mist and an overcast sky which was gradually breaking into patches of blue.

'I don't believe it.'

Her voice was weak with exhaustion. 'I've checked on your father. He's awake and in some pain, but I don't think he's any worse.'

It was cool among the trees, and the fire and the hostile vehicles and the young man with the gun seemed a long way away.

'What about Paco?'

'He's still wheezing. They're under the oaks.' She gestured towards three figures in the long grass a few metres away. 'I've been to the farm.'

Alex felt guilty at having fallen so soundly asleep.

'The man at the security gate was Mexican. He told

me there *are* vacancies and no one bothers about papers. We have to go back at ten and he's promised to help your father.' Cristina didn't use his name, as if she wanted to put Steve at a distance.

'It sounds too perfect,' said Alex. 'Too neat and easy.'

'Maybe it is. But we have to take our chance.'

'I'll go and check on Dad. I'm sorry I fell asleep.'

She leant over and kissed him.

His father lay next to Paco and Maria. They looked like sleeping warriors. Then Steve's eyes opened slowly.

'Alex...'

'Are you in pain?'

'Yes.'

He was surprised. For the first time Steve had given him a straight answer. 'Cristina's fixed up a doctor to see you, but not until ten.'

'Am I going to be all right? My arm hurts like hell.'

'You'll be fine.' Alex winced at his glib reassurance, dragging his mind away from the dreadful thought that his father might die. A line from a poem he had read at school swam into his head. *The child is father of the man.* He'd never really understood it before. Now he did. 'Shall I stay with you?'

'Go and check on Paco. I'll last out.' He sounded doubtful.

'Of course you will,' Alex said with what he knew was a false optimism.

He was sure that Cristina would say, once again, that he was just like his father. Well – so what if he was?

Paco's breathing was definitely less laboured as Alex nudged him awake. Eventually he stirred, gazing at Alex blankly for a moment.

'We're here – at the farm – and there's work. You're safe.'

But, like Steve, Paco didn't look convinced.

'You're safe,' Alex repeated. 'You're in California. Come and take a look.'

The two boys walked up the trail to a small rise and then plunged down into a long, low tunnel overhung by gnarled pines and thick brush. Through gaps in the pine canopy they caught glimpses of the Otay Mesa and then, suddenly, the blue of the Pacific. As the trail wound uphill again, Paco and Alex could see the ocean more clearly, the waves pounding at a beach humped with sand dunes.

'Can you breathe more easily now?' In fact Paco's shoulders were heaving again, but then they had been walking uphill for some minutes. 'Let's take a rest and watch the waves.'

Paco slowly sank down beside Alex, clasping his knees.

'Will you come back and see us?'

'You bet.' Alex was conscious that yet again he sounded too assertive, too optimistic. He couldn't lie to Paco. He was the only person he had been truthful with.

After all, they were brothers, weren't they? 'Neither of us knows what's going to happen,' Alex admitted, his anxiety rising. 'Do you think my father will want to stay here?'

'And pick oranges? I don't think so.'

'Why not?'

'Steve must go home with you. That's where he belongs.'

But did he? That was the problem, thought Alex. His father didn't seem to belong anywhere. He glimpsed his mother, scarf flying in the wind, trailing down to the village shops with the shabby old basket on wheels, her face set against the kind of lifestyle Steve represented.

Back at the truck, they found a middle-aged Mexican talking to Cristina and Maria in Spanish. Judging by their expressions, he didn't think they were receiving particularly good news.

'What's happening?' asked Alex.

'Felipe is telling us how bad conditions are on the farm and explaining how much better off we'd all be in Tijuana,' said Cristina woodenly. 'What about a doctor?' she asked him in English.

For the first time Felipe seemed to have better news. 'He's good. I broke my foot. He fixed it OK.'

Paco pulled the watch Alex had given him out of his pocket and gazed at it.

'You ought to wear that round your wrist,' Alex reminded him.

Paco shook his head. 'I might break it.'

As Cristina started to drag the rucksacks out of the truck, Steve called out to her.

'Is everything going to be all right?' he asked like a frightened child.

'Yes.' Cristina's voice was kind but neutral. 'It's going to be all right.' She glanced across at Alex, looking as if she had been caught out.

Alex went to his father and tried to help him up, but Steve pushed him away. 'I'll manage on my own,' he muttered.

Alex realised he couldn't bear to be touched. The pain was too great. He saw Cristina drop another marigold petal and wondered if it was her last.

The small procession that walked up the road to the farm seemed, to Alex, both pathetic and bizarre.

Cristina and Maria walked together, followed by Steve, staggering, clasping his arm again but still refusing any help from Paco and Alex who flanked him on either side.

The sun was an orange blob high above their heads in a cloudless sky and gave a gentle warming heat. Gulls mewed above their heads.

Then Paco stopped and pointed.

'Is that a dove?'

Alex scanned the sky but saw only gulls.

'I said he'd come as a dove.'

'Who?' demanded Alex, too exhausted to understand, watching his father weave erratically, looking as if he might fall down at any moment.

'Luis. I told you. He's here. He followed the marigold path.'

Cristina and Maria turned round, coming to an abrupt halt.

'*Que?*'

Paco spoke to them in English for Alex's benefit. 'I saw a dove.'

They both looked up at the sky but they too saw only the gulls. But their faces showed how happy they felt.

'I saw Luis,' Paco insisted.

Before any more could be said, Steve staggered across the road to a patch of grass in front of the farm gates and collapsed, somehow managing to turn himself on to his side. But when Alex rushed over and knelt beside him, his father was unconscious and he could do nothing to rouse him.

'Get the doctor,' he yelled.

Paco began to run towards the gates. Then Alex glanced up. Above his head a dove was hovering. He heard a cooing sound and then the bird began to fly after Paco.

'Luis,' wept Cristina, but Maria was already kneeling by Steve and taking his hand.

'Thank you,' she whispered.

FIFTEEN

Alex sat on the steps of the first aid post and gazed miserably out at the rows of orange trees under the cobalt blue sky. He knew that he had to face the very real possibility that his father might die. He tried to push away the appalling idea. Dad was no longer stranger Steve. He was Dad. Father. Someone who had returned from a long series of journeys away from him. Someone Alex now loved deeply.

From the early rejection at the hotel to the romantic adventure of the shanty town, from the blind courage on the Otay Mesa to the need to be wanted when Paco nearly died, his father seemed to have emerged as both hero and villain. There was a bond between them now that no one could destroy. Yet Alex was deepy afraid – frightened that he was about to lose his father for ever.

The thoughts couldn't be driven away so, instead, he watched a minute humming bird flying like a hovercraft, alighting on the branch of a small twisted pine tree, colours almost as subtle as a butterfly.

'I'm breathing easier.' Paco was standing beside him, looking around furtively.

'You're going to get well here.'

'The wages are low.' He broke off. 'How is Steve?'

'I'm waiting for the ambulance. They can't help him here. He needs to have an operation in the hospital.' Alex tried to speak calmly.

'He's going to be all right, isn't he?'

'Of course.'

There was a long pause and then Paco said, 'You sound like him.'

Alex almost broke down. 'Actually – I don't know if he's going to be all right.'

'I'm sure he'll be OK.'

'Now *you* sound like him.'

They both laughed uneasily. Then they heard the ambulance siren.

'One day we'll go down to the ocean. I'd like to surf. Can you teach me?' asked Paco.

'I'm not much good,' said Alex. 'It would be like the football.'

'Does that matter?'

They shook hands as the ambulance appeared, blue lights flashing. Then Paco hugged him. 'Goodbye, brother,' he said.

* * *

Steve seemed to be weakening in the swaying ambulance and a paramedic gave him oxygen. He didn't speak at all and, as Alex sat on the opposite bunk and watched him, neither of the paramedics said he was going to be OK.

For some strange reason this brought him comfort. The truth was needed now and all the lies and evasions had to stop.

But if the doctors *did* save his father's life, would he and Mum have a chance at last? A chance to start all over again? He felt torn between them both; his father with his need to control, to invent a life and his mother, hurt and rejected, too frightened to offer help.

At the hospital just outside San Diego, Steve was rushed into the Emergency Room while Alex was led to a waiting area. A nurse brought him coffee and a hamburger which he ate ravenously.

Hours passed like days as he waited for the door to open at any moment, admitting a grim-faced doctor bearing terrible news. But when she did come it was an anti-climax for she was smiling. Was this a professional smile, or could it be genuine?

'He's come through surgery, but your father's lost a lot of blood.' She paused. 'And I'm sorry – there's an infection too.'

'You think he'll make it?'

The doctor, who was young and crisp and efficient, said quickly, 'We don't know yet. We're doing everything we can. Do you want to see him for a few minutes? Then I can let you have a bed here, unless you've got anywhere else to go?'

'I haven't,' insisted Alex fiercely.

'Alex?' he whispered. His face was withered and the texture of grey wool.

'I'm here, Dad.'

'I'm sorry.'

'What for?'

'Making a mess of things.'

'You got them across – and me, too.'

'How's Paco?'

'Better.'

'Thank God. I'm not going to leave you, Alex. You know what I mean, don't you?'

'I know what you mean, Dad. You're not to do that. Not ever again.'

Alex could barely hear his father as he whispered, 'I won't.'

Then he remembered the dove. 'Dad – do I have to call you Steve any more?'

His father shook his head and smiled weakly.

'There's something else.'

'What?'

Alex could see a nurse hovering and knew he had to be quick. 'We saw a dove.'

'So?'

'Paco thinks it was Luis.'

'Maybe it was.'

Before he went to bed, Alex was able to phone home. He had already decided what he was going to say as he stood in the office while a nurse dialled the number.

She left discreetly when his mother answered and Alex began the story he had made up for her. *You sound like your father.* Paco's voice beat in his mind. He wondered if his mother was thinking the same.

'You're not to worry, Mum.'

'What's happened?' She was immediately suspicious. Alex could also hear a curious drumming sound.

'What's that?'

'Rain. It's pouring down. What's happened?'

'Dad's had an accident, but he's going to be OK.' Alex didn't want to tell her anything else now. He was too exhausted.

'What sort of accident?'

'Car.'

'Are you all right?'

'I'm fine.'

'You're sure?'

'Really fine. He's had an operation...'

'As bad as that?'

'But the doctor says he's going to be all right.'

'Where are you phoning from?'

'The hospital at San Diego.'

'I *knew* you should never have gone out there.'

'I've learnt a lot.'

'What about?'

'Dad.'

Alex spent the next day wandering the hospital corridors, eating in the canteen, watching TV in his room and sitting at his father's bedside, watching him struggle against the infection. For a long time he seemed to make no progress at all and the nurses said very little, the doctors nothing at all.

Time seemed to be on hold and to become dream-like as Alex relived the Day of the Dead, still wondering if the Grim Reaper was going to claim a life. He remembered being on the dump with Paco, listening to his wheezing, watching the fence posts that were burnt animals, imagining Luis being washed out of his grave.

But Alex also thought of the football match, the party in the shanty town, Cristina's admiration for him on the Mesa and he realised that for the first time he had felt a sense of purpose, of acceptance.

Then he was besieged by his mother's fierce love and he knew that he didn't want to blame her. He missed her desperately and would have done anything to be back with her, walking past marsh and shingle, heading for the shop where she loved to talk, to be safe, to be secure in the way she had to be.

On the second morning, the nurse knocked on the door of his small cubicle-like bedroom – and the Day of the Dead reached out to Alex again.

'There's a cop come to see you,' she said.

'What about?'

'Your father.'

'Has something happened. Is he—'

'No, no. He's doing OK. It's about your father's accident.'

Panic welled inside him as he realised he should have made up some kind of story a long time ago, just like he had for Mum.

'Get dressed and grab some breakfast. The officer has to see another patient first. There's no hurry.'

He was middle-aged and appeared kind, but Alex was sure the kindness was a trick. He hoped the story he had made up would somehow be accepted. But suppose his father was interviewed? The stories wouldn't hang together at all. Ironically, it would be better if he was still too ill to be seen.

The interview room was hostile and cheerless, with its scratched table, plastic chairs and a picture of the Niagara Falls at a slight angle on the wall. For some reason, Alex longed to straighten it up.

'Call me Bob, Alex.'

'OK.' For a moment the police officer sounded absurdly like his father.

'It must be hard with your dad so sick.'

'Yes.'

'You called your Mom and put her in the picture?'

He nodded.

'She must be worried out of her mind.'

Alex nodded again, his nerves making him tongue-tied.

'So how did your father get this gunshot wound?'

'We went for a drive. We wanted to talk. We weren't getting on so well.' Alex was conscious that his voice was too clipped. Did it sound as if he had been carefully rehearsing?

'Why was that?'

'He was thinking of leaving my mother. Staying out here.'

'Your dad's a photographer?'

'Yes.'

'Was he working on something?'

'I'm not sure.'

'So you went for a drive. What time was that?'

'Early, about six, I think.'

'Where did you drive?'

'In the hills.'

'There are a lot of hills round here.' He smiled, but

from Alex's point of view rather threateningly.

'I'm not sure which ones. Anyway, there was this bush fire and Dad had to drive fast to get away from it.'

'That sounds like the border.'

'Does it?' Alex's mind was leaping ahead protectively, not just for his father but for Cristina and Paco and Maria as well. It didn't look as if the people at the fruit farm had said anything – but he couldn't be sure. Bob was an enemy. Just like the young vigilante. 'Anyway – we got stopped on this track.'

'Who by?'

'A guy in a jeep. He held us up. He wanted money.'

'What did he look like?'

Alex's thoughts raced and he could almost hear the deep, incriminating silence.

'Don't you recall?'

'Yes. I'm just trying to be accurate. Trying to remember the exact details.'

'Take your time.'

The face of an actor playing in a corny cowboy film he had seen last night on TV flashed into his mind. 'He was tall with a long narrow face and a little beard on the point of his chin. Apart from that he was clean-shaven, and middle-aged. He had an earring and—'

Alex came to a grinding halt for he was about to add that he had been wearing a broad-brimmed hat. But that would have been *too* ridiculous.

'That's all I can remember about him.'

The officer nodded, but he couldn't work out whether he believed him or not.

'What happened next?'

'This guy pulled open the door. Dad turned to face him and he just pulled the trigger and shot him.'

'Was the truck moving at the time?'

'No.'

'And then?'

'Dad got it going again and we drove off.'

'Despite being injured?'

'He still drove,' Alex said doggedly.

'Where to?' The police officer's smile reminded him of Oscar's fixed grin.

'We were going back to the Del Coronado where we were staying. Then Dad said his arm hurt bad so we stopped off at this farm and they called an ambulance.'

'That's it?'

'It's all I can remember.'

'I should have been here yesterday, but there was some kind of communications problem between the hospital and us. The shooting's only just got reported.'

Alex felt at least some temporary relief. So a mistake had been made and the trail had gone cold. That should protect Cristina.

'We're going to start looking for this guy, but it's kind of late. Anything else you can remember about him?'

Alex pretended to wrack his brains and then had a sudden thought. He had already lied. Why not lie some more? Guiltily, he realised his father should be proud of him. 'Wait a minute.'

'Yeah?' The officer's eyes were on his now.

'He had a tattoo on his arm. He was wearing a torn T-shirt and there was this tattoo. I can't think how I'd forgotten.' He tried to sound excited, hoping to make himself more convincing.

'What kind of tattoo?'

Alex's mind almost dried up again. 'It was a spider,' he said suddenly. 'A great big hairy spider.'

'OK.' The officer picked up his notebook and read it back.

'We have a guy who is tall with a long narrow face. Middle-aged with a small beard on the point of his chin with an earring and a spider tattoo on his arm.' He paused. 'Are you done?'

'Yes.' Panic filled Alex. His father *had* to corroborate the story. But how could he? Suppose the cop got to him first? Would Cristina and Maria and Paco be deported? Alex was terrified his lies would be unravelled and the truth uncovered. It would be entirely his fault.

The officer stood up. Had he been convincing, or had he just made him sceptical?

'You sure you're telling me the truth, son?'

Alex began to sweat. 'Of course I am.'

'You know we'll check your story out?'

'I *want* you to.' Never had he felt more insincere.

There was a long, awkward silence.

'This has been a bad experience for you,' the officer said slowly, and Alex wondered if he was on safer ground. 'We'll try to get this guy, and I'll come back and talk to your dad when he's better.' He paused. 'And you, Alex.' The threat had returned.

They shook hands.

When he had gone, Alex wondered if the officer had noticed how sweaty his palm had been. Suddenly he was sure he had.

He tried to see his father but the nurse wouldn't let him in.

'The doctor's there,' she said, but he knew by the look in her eyes that there was something badly wrong.

'What's happening?' Alex asked woodenly.

'The infection's got worse. There's resistance to the antibiotic. We're doing all we can.'

He went down to the shop in the hospital foyer and then, unable to bear being inside any longer, walked out into mellow sunshine. A road led downhill and there was a bus stop and a gently sloping canyon filled with lush grass and flowers and trees. By the roadside the grass had been smoothly cut and a rotating spray ensured its perfection.

Just above the rise, the skyscrapers of San Diego gleamed golden in the sunlight.

Alex felt as if he had arrived in hell, richly disguised as heaven.

He walked up and down the road for a while, feeling a slow surge of grief and despair for the father he had hardly known but had come to love so much.

No longer able to hold back the tears, he walked into the long grass of the canyon and hid himself behind a tree, burying his face in his hands and sobbing so hard that he ached inside.

Alex looked up to see a young Mexican gardener clasping a bucket.

'Something wrong?'

'I'm fine.'

'OK. Excuse me.' He looked embarrassed and turned away.

'My father's in the hospital. He's very ill.' Alex didn't want him to feel shut out or patronised.

'I'll pray for him.'

They gazed at each other awkwardly and Alex felt the need to fill the silence. 'What's in the can?'

'Chemicals. That's the way they treat the grass here. They keep away the weeds. Once this canyon was as bare as the hills above Tijuana, but the Americans sowed seeds and made the land green. They pipe in the water from another state. They make their paradise.' He paused and then asked, 'Do you know Mexico?'

'A little.' Alex didn't want to talk any longer. He wanted to be on his own. As he walked slowly back towards the road he could hear the young Mexican calling after him: 'I'll pray for your father.'

He telephoned his mother, giving her a fictionalised account of Steve's slow recovery. She seemed satisfied.

Walking back to his room, Alex took a different route through the hospital, finding another shop which was packed with books and mementos of Mexico's Day of the Dead. He examined a plastic skeleton and then a cardboard house with its windows wide open to receive the souls of the dead children. In the downstairs room a cardboard cut-out family sat around a cardboard table piled high with cardboard offerings.

Eventually, Alex went to his room and was just about to turn on the TV when the internal telephone rang. He froze. Had his father died? He sat on his bed, unable to move. Then he grabbed the receiver.

'Alex Carson?'

'Yes.'

She *was* going to say he was dead. He *knew* she was going to say he was dead.

'Would you like to come up and see your dad?'

'I've been so afraid.' Steve's voice was weak and he seemed to have aged since Alex had last seen him.

'What have you been afraid of?' He sat down by the bed and took his father's hand. The palm was hot and sweaty, just as Alex's had been when he shook hands with the police officer.

'I couldn't find you. I didn't know where you were.'

'I've been here all the time, waiting in the hospital.'

'You were lost on the Mesa.'

'I'm not lost, Dad. I'm here.'

'You'll go away.'

'You've been ill. You're getting better.'

His father closed his eyes. Then, after a long while and just when Alex was thinking of leaving, he spoke again.

'I want to come home.'

Was he telling the truth, Alex wondered. Wasn't this more likely to be delirium? And what about the police? His father might be arrested if they found out what he had really done. He would have to brief him carefully.

'I want to come home,' Steve repeated.

'OK, Dad,' Alex said. Then, 'I'd like to see Paco. Can we do that when you're better?'

His father nodded, suddenly drained.

SIXTEEN

Ten days later.

As Steve drove back to the fruit farm in a rented car, Alex was concerned about how weak he still looked.

'We've got to sort it out, Dad.'

'Sort what out?'

'How you're going to live with me and Mum.'

At once Steve was indignant. 'What do you mean? I'm your dad. Your mother is my wife.'

'But you've never treated us like that. How *are* you going to make it work?' Alex paused. 'And how are we? I don't want to push you away again and neither will Mum.'

'I'm not *going* away.'

'You've got a living to earn. You can't sit at home all the time.' He paused and then asked, 'What's *Atlas* magazine going to say about you losing their money?'

'I'll tell them the truth. We're all in the risk business.'

'Suppose they ask you to pay all those dollars back?'

'I can't.' Steve grinned. 'You can't get blood out of a stone.'

'You lost plenty of blood too,' muttered Alex.

His father gave Alex a surprised glance. 'You've grown up a bit, haven't you?'

'So have you.'

'All right.' Steve Carson laughed, but not with much humour. 'Let's call it quits. I know we've got to work at it – all three of us. I realise Cristina and I were only using each other. Like one hell of a lot. But I do feel some responsibility for her. I don't know if she gives a damn about me, though. She probably hasn't given me a single thought, couldn't care less whether I lived or died.' Steve paused, drawing back from the edge of becoming maudlin. 'Anyway – it's a good thing, isn't it?'

'That we're going to see them? I think so.'

'Get it over with,' said his father. 'After all, we're flying home tomorrow.'

Alex suddenly realised how much Steve wanted to move on. But it won't be as easy as that, he thought.

Alex was amazed at the poor conditions Cristina, Maria and Paco were living in. Although the farm was much cleaner than the shanty town, and there was no pollution in the clear Californian air, the family had no privacy. They were camping in cramped conditions with the other Mexican workers in a series of battered old greenhouses, roughly converted into makeshift living quarters.

As his father held a stiff and awkward conversation with Cristina and Maria, Paco and Alex walked down to a nearby dried-out creek. They stood on its dusty bank looking down into the trickle of brackish-looking water.

'Your breathing seems easier,' said Alex.

'It is. That's California.' Paco was determined to be optimistic.

'I don't think much of where you're living.'

'It's all he can give us. He's a small farmer and he's dropped out of the system.'

'What system?' asked Alex.

'The big farmers only hire legal workers and they have to build good housing for them. But Saul Jackson, he can't afford to do that. He can't *afford* to have legal workers. So he's got us. And we live like this. It's still better than the dump.'

Alex had to agree that it was. But was this place really worth all the dangers of getting across the border?

Then Steve yelled out that it was time they were getting back.

Alex held out his hand. 'I'll stay in touch. I'll write. I'll find out the address and write.'

'That wouldn't be such a good idea,' said Paco. 'We're not meant to exist. Right?'

'Right,' said Alex. 'But I'll keep in touch somehow. Without giving you away.' He scribbled down his address on a piece of paper and gave it to him. 'Let me know how things are going,' Alex pleaded.

He watched Paco in the wing mirror as they drove away, his figure getting smaller and smaller.

Paco made no attempt to wave but just stood there staring. Then Alex saw the paper flutter to the ground as Paco turned and walked away. The hurt began to spread inside Alex, burning up into this throat, and he swallowed hard. His world had moved on, and now he had a new relationship with his father. He must try to hold on to that.

A dove rose up in front of them dazzling white against the blue sky. Alex followed its flight until he could see it no longer, lost in the brilliance of the California sunlight.

Also by Anthony Masters

'*There is no doubt that Anthony Masters knows how to pack a story full of fast-moving incidents, sharply drawn characters and emotional turmoil.*' Junior Bookshelf

Wicked
Josh's brothers are hiding a secret – one so terrible that it's tearing them apart. Josh wants the truth...but is he ready for it?

'*Suspension is stretched almost to breaking point...there is a nightmare quality that is both gripping and believable.*' Nicholas Tucker, The Independent

Spinner
Gary is locked in an autistic world: one that Jane longs to be part of, longs to understand. Witnesses to a brutal crime, they are in grave danger and Jane must protect Gary at all costs.

'*An exciting thriller.*' Junior Bookshelf

Also by Anthony Masters

GHOSTHUNTERS series
Spooky apparitions appear when ghosthunters
Jenny and David are around. . .